"Justin."

"—you've done nothing but offer your unasked-for opinions ever since you arrived here. You've been criticizing everything you see, but—"

"Lydie..."

"—I'd appreciate it if you didn't criticize *me*."

"Hold still," he murmured.

"What?"

As she glared at him, uncomprehending, he reached across the bed. His face was suddenly quite close to hers; his fingers brushed her hair. Startled, she stared at him, then looked down to see the furry strip of green on his forefinger.

"Someone about to visit your left ear," Justin said softly.

Lydie bent forward, her anger arrested as she looked at the beautiful, tiny caterpillar.

"Didn't mean to disturb you," Justin murmured, seeming to address the agitated creature. But Lydie sensed the apology hovering behind those playful words.

When she looked up, his eyes seemed perilously close, their dark velvet depths glimmering with gold flecks of inviting warmth...

Lee Williams

Lee Williams has been writing—books, plays, song lyrics, and librettos—practically since she learned how to print. Her first attempt was a play, which she wrote and directed when she was in second grade. Unfortunately, it never made it to the Harbor Road School stage, having been replaced by unscrupulous adults with a Fourth of July pageant. Undaunted, in junior high Lee went on to film her own 8mm movie silents, starring classmates. When these didn't yield a Hollywood contract, she began to produce poems and short stories.

Lee didn't set out to become a writer of romances, but having penned the lyrics for many a pop love song, she found it a natural extension. "The one thing common to every writing medium," she muses, "is romance. There's always a man or a woman, whether we're speaking of Shakespeare, a musical comedy, or a SECOND CHANCE AT LOVE book. The tiniest moment of erotic eye contact can yield the most fascinating complications..."

Lee lives with her husband and a large family of felines in Manhattan's Greenwich Village. At the moment, she's juggling half a dozen projects, including a musical-in-progress and two screenplays.

Other Second Chance at Love books by
Lee Williams

Dear Reader:

For all you Kay Robbins fans, here's a brand-new reason to cheer: *Belonging to Taylor* (#322). Beautiful psychic Taylor Shannon knows Trevor King is the man she's destined to marry. But, as any self-respecting male would, Trevor has his doubts about "belonging" to *anyone*. Told by the beleaguered hero as he manfully resists seduction, *Belonging to Taylor* offers all the wit and whimsy you've come to expect from Kay Robbins ... and a serious exploration of the wondrous meaning of true love. Humorous and dramatic, playful and poignant, *Belonging to Taylor* is a romance to cherish.

A high-tech genius may not be the usual stuff of which heroes are made, but in *Anywhere and Always* (#323) by Lee Williams, brilliant, offbeat Justin Fuller is a quintessential heartthrob. Arriving in Lydie Henley's hometown for an enforced vacation, Justin astounds her with inventive wizardry, catches her off-guard with amazing insights, and completely sweeps her away. How can she resist a man who so eagerly anticipates her lessons in "How to Relax Away From a Computer"? How can she say no to a disheveled sweetheart who's apt to forget to go to bed ... unless she's there to entice him? *Anywhere and Always* will leave you with a smile and a sigh.

In *Fortune's Choice* (#324), Elissa Curry pairs another of her "bad boy" heroes, handsome rogue Nick Parmenter, with slightly spoiled socialite "Joey" Fortune, whose father has finally tied the purse strings and thrust her out into the cold, cold world. What's more logical than for two such ne'er-do-wells to join forces in a risky venture—selling ice cream? Of course, they survive poverty in high style *and* contend with a slimy fortune-hunter, some wily gangsters, and a resourceful priest. Reading *Fortune's Choice* is like watching a 1930's romantic comedy. Hepburn and Tracy, move over!

I'm thrilled to introduce Cait Logan, a talented newcomer whose *Lady on the Line* (#325) may remind you of the work of another of our popular authors, Ann

Cristy. Like Ann, Cait Logan creates the larger-than-life heroes we all dream about—men who are masculine in *every* sense of the word. Barrett Redding makes K.C. Bollins feel *very* womanly, and he wants nothing more than to protect her. But K.C. is used to taking care of herself and her son, to surviving in a tough world. Yet she's scorched by the heat of Barrett's hungry gaze ... *Lady on the Line* is a real sizzler!

Seldom do women *like* turning forty, and the heroine of *A Kiss Away* (#326) by Sherryl Woods is no exception. Jessica Warren plans to greet the big "four-oh" with a dose of maturity *and* a physically fit body. But her new exercise plan sends her limping into the sympathetic—and irritatingly muscular—arms of her gorgeous neighbor, Kevin Lawrence. In no time Kevin's boyish energy, disregard for propriety, and shamelessly erotic pursuit have Jessica's hormones hopping. Sherryl Woods brings us both humor and a mature love story.

If you thrill to the stories of the silver screen, then *Play It Again, Sam* (#327) by Petra Diamond is the romance for you. To incurably nostalgic Nedda Shaw, Brooklyn-born costume designer Sam Harrison is about as foreign as they come. Sam brazenly vows to drag Nedda kicking into the twentieth century—and his bed—but he soon learns that the only way to a Southern belle's body is through her heart. As Sam gamely attempts an old-fashioned courtship, both he and Nedda are perplexed, and thrilled, to discover true love!

Until next month, warmest wishes,

Ellen Edwards

Ellen Edwards, Senior Editor
SECOND CHANCE AT LOVE
The Berkley Publishing Group
200 Madison Avenue
New York, NY 10016

LEE WILLIAMS
ANYWHERE AND ALWAYS

A
SECOND CHANCE AT LOVE
BOOK

Second Chance at Love books are published by
The Berkley Publishing Group
200 Madison Avenue, New York, NY 10016

CHAPTER ONE

Sɪᴘᴘɪɴɢ ᴛʜᴇ ᴄᴏʟᴅ apple cider as a welcome breeze caressed her face, Lydie Henley decided that for the moment, life was good. The cider was fresh from an oaken barrel at Mr. McCready's produce stand on Route 22, and the breeze was strong, wafting with it the faint scent of cherries from a nearby orchard.

Lydie lifted the material of her white button-down from where it had stuck to her back and lifted her face, eyes closed, to savor the sun for a moment as the tartness of the cider soaked into her tongue.

You've done it, she told herself with a little swell of pride. It may have taken nearly two months, but you've finally succeeded in getting seven years of harried, hassled, and hysterical city life out of your system . . . at least temporarily.

A bark from Scruff made her open her eyes again. The red-haired retriever was scratching at the door of her car, ears up at the crackling static of the radio. Her dispatcher was calling with another fare. "Hold on, Marge," Lydie murmured. She finished off the little jug of cider, and reached into her jeans for some silver.

She was the only customer at McCready's at the moment. McCready himself was off fishing. Lydie walked over to the open notebook on the wooden stand, picked up the stub of a pencil marking its open page, and made a note of the transaction: "cider, small size." Then she opened the rusty metal cashbox, dropped in four quarters and a dime, extracted her penny change, and shut the box again.

McCready's was run on the honor system. For a brief moment, as she sauntered back to her battered but dependable navy-blue Volvo, Lydie tried to imagine how a place like this would fare back in New York City. The idea brought a rueful smile to her lips. If McCready had tried it on her old block, west of Central Park in the upper Eighties, he'd be lucky to find the pencil there at the end of his first business day. Let alone the cashbox or a solitary ear of corn.

Lydie opened the door, let Scruff lurch ahead onto the seat, and then climbed in. She palmed the little microphone that dangled from the dashboard and clicked it on. "Big Marge," she said. "This is the Wanderer. What's up?"

After a moment, Marjorie's cigarette-hoarse voice came crackling over the speaker. "Hey, Wander Woman. Where are you?"

"McCready's." Lydie yawned. "Got another confused fez-head?"

Marge chuckled. "You sure do have a way with words, Lydie. No, they're all over at the Mayflower, I guess, doing whatever they do with those silly-looking hats." The Shriners were having a convention in Traverse City, and there had been many calls for cabs before noon. "No, I need for you to swing by the airport. There's a fellow there wants to go to your hometown, Lord knows why."

Scruff barked, his nose sniffing at the speaker as if in disdain at this slight to his stomping grounds, then scrambled into the back seat. Lydie chuckled, patting his head. "Hear that, Marge? Birchwood's finest doesn't take kindly to slander. What've you got against the place, anyway?"

"Bunch of loons live around that part of the lake, Lydie."

"Start calling us names and Scruff'll do more than just bark at you," Lydie said in a tone of mock affrontedness. "Loons, indeed. Just because my town has a reputation for going a little wild at the end of tourist season—"

"—and plumb stir crazy by the end of the winter—"

"—is no reason to characterize the entire population as funny-farm fodder," Lydie said. "And you used to live there yourself, remember? So skip the opinions and just tell me who to look for. Tall, fat, skinny—?"

"His name's Fuller, and he's waiting in front. Think you can get there before sundown?"

Fuller? As the name registered, Lydie felt a sudden jolt of irritation. "Oh, no," she exclaimed. "He's here? Already?"

"Friend of yours?" inquired Marge.

"No," Lydie sighed. "All right, I'm on my way. I'll check in when I've picked him up."

She clicked the radio off, craning her neck out her side window as she prepared to make a U-turn. A few cars passed, toting boats and carrying weekend vacationers. Scruff was looking anxiously out the other window, a canine parody of a backseat driver. Lydie gunned the motor and swung the car in a graceful arc.

So much for a feeling of blissful well-being. Justin Fuller wasn't supposed to be arriving until tomorrow morning. It was bad enough that he was coming at all, but early? Lydie stifled a groan. This formerly idyllic day was taking a sudden turn for the worse.

Dad had gotten the call from Willy Koska a week ago. Fuller, a business acquaintance of his son Pete's, was looking for a bucolic hideway. Pete had thought of the Henleys' place, on the off chance it wasn't already rented. Well, it wasn't, for once, mainly because Lydie herself had taken it for the summer. But since she wasn't about to deny her family a chance to make some money, she was moving herself out of it and into the farmhouse in preparation for this Justin Fuller's arrival.

But she wasn't done clearing the cabin out. And though the family had welcomed her warmly when she'd shown up on the doorstep unannounced, she wasn't enthusiastic about moving in with them, dears that they were. She'd been looking forward to one last night of solitude and privacy. . . .

The airport, all of a half-block of building in front of a football-field-sized tarmac, was already in view through the windshield. Lydie picked up her baseball cap from the worn upholstery and set it atop her unkempt auburn hair. She pulled the visor down to shade her face from the midafternoon sun and squinted, frowning.

What was he doing, coming up on the last Sunday in August? Most of the summer people were winding up their vacations. She and everyone else in town were looking forward to the tourists' mass exodus on the upcoming Labor Day weekend. And now some lone Sunday fisherman was usurping her place.

She pulled up to the curb outside the terminal. No one was waiting there. Lydie flicked her radio on again. "Marge, I don't see anyone. Call came from the airport?"

"Sure did, Lydie."

"He must be inside, then, waiting for all the luggage he didn't need to bring. You know those guys that fly in from the city. I can just picture him, dressed right out of an L. L. Bean catalog, all revved up and desperate to unwind. Pale skin ready to burn—"

"Lydie Henley," Marge interrupted. "You've only been back here for eight weeks, and already you sound as persnickety as the locals."

"You're right," Lydie allowed, chagrined.

"And when you first came back you were pretty critical of this place."

"Was I? Hard to believe," she said ruefully. "You know, I was just thinking that I don't miss New York at all anymore."

"Really? Well, you must miss *something* about it . . . like that place you told me about—what was it, Chippendale's?"

Lydie laughed. Marjorie and her cronies had been fascinated by Lydie's reports of the city's new male striptease club, catering to women only. "Marge, I swear to you. The last thing I miss about New York City is the men," Lydie said wryly.

"Now, you can't rule them *all* out, honey."

"Sure I can," she said firmly. "If I've learned anything, it's that me and relationships just don't mix."

"You just wait till the right man comes around,

Lydie," Marge said in her best motherly tone. "You'll be mixed up and matched up before you know it."

"No way," Lydie protested. "I'm not waiting for any man—except this one, wherever he is." She sighed. "I'd better go inside and lend him a hand with his stuff, if that's what's keeping him."

"Good girl. Call me when you hit Birchwood."

Lydie walked through the terminal doors. Hands on the hips of her blue jeans, she paused, stretching her back, and peered about the cool interior. Not exactly a bustling axis of travel and commerce, this, she mused wryly, automatically comparing the all-but-deserted airport to the seething hysteria of LaGuardia in New York. Now, where was Mr. Fuller?

Scanning the ticket counter area, one-ramp baggage claim, and waiting room, her eyes came to an abrupt halt at the lone public phone booth in the corner. There was a small crowd gathered there. If her ears didn't deceive her, someone was playing music.

Street musicians? In a northern Michigan airport? Curious, Lydie sauntered over. She could hear single high notes on what sounded like a pitch pipe, and then enthusiastic applause from the onlookers—two kids and their mom, some teenagers, an elderly man, and a terminal attendant, broom in hand. Peering over the heads of the younger folks, she saw a sight that was even more confounding.

There was a man seated on a suitcase by the booth. He had a toy harmonica—a red plastic one—poised in his fingers, and a gently whirring machine at his feet. A few feet of coiled wire snaked from the machine to the telephone.

Lydie stared at the man, puzzled, feeling a little jolt of indefinable excitement as she took in his features. *Handsome* was too tame a word to describe him. He looked like . . . a civilized Pan, with the pipe at his lips and sensuous mischief in his gleaming eyes.

Those eyes met Lydie's. Their dark depths seemed to lock into crisp focus suddenly, pulling her in with a magnetic force. Lydie had a vivid, intuitive flash that she might be in trouble.

With the disconcertingly direct gaze came a disarmingly attractive array of other features, including a strong chin, a full-lipped smile, an aquiline nose, and sexily disheveled thick black hair complete with a curly shock of it falling over his eyes. His body was long, his shoulders broad, and his expression one of amused interest that instantly put her on the defensive.

Justin Fuller. She knew it had to be he. His black penny loafers, brown corduroys, and simple but well-tailored powder-blue shirt suggested city slicker, all the way. But what in God's name was he up to?

Lydie realized that she'd been smiling back at the man unconsciously—perhaps the reason for the interested look glimmering in those come-hither eyes. She forced her mouth into a frown and broke eye contact, looking with unfeigned curiosity at the machine at his feet. It obviously was some kind of a computer.

So he had the kind of looks that made her insides turn to jelly. For all she knew, he could be some kind of crackpot.

Next to him, a skin-headed serviceman in uniform was standing in the booth, the wired phone receiver at his ear and a broad grin on his face. "Yeah, we just got in," he was saying. "I tried to call and the phone was broke—but this guy fixed it."

Not a crackpot, then. But . . . what?

"I wanna make a call!" One of the kids, a curly-blond-haired little boy, tugged at his mother's skirt.

Justin Fuller smiled. "Sure. It's your harmonica," he said, holding up the plastic instrument. "You're entitled. I'll dial for you next."

"Thanks, mister." The serviceman was done with his call, and was holding the receiver out to Justin.

"You're welcome. Okay, now..."

"Steven," supplied the boy.

"... Steven, tell me the phone number you want to call."

"Three-six-two..." He checked with his mother. "Four-three-one-one. That's our house."

Justin nodded, and his fingers made a brief flurry over the small computer keyboard in front of him. Then, holding the harmonica to his lips, he blew a series of notes toward a little square grille in the machine, his eyes on the blond-haired boy.

Grinning excitedly, the blond-haired boy listened, clutching the wired receiver to his ear. "It's ringing!" he exclaimed, and once again the onlookers applauded, making murmurs of appreciation. "Hi, Dad! It's me—Steven."

Lydie glanced at the dial of the pay phone; it was twisted out of shape. She was no technological wizard. She could only surmise that the man had found some creative way to get past the broken apparatus.

Impressed, she regarded her new cabin tenant with interest as he rose to his feet and began packing up the computer. Lydie watched the man accept the teenagers' accolades with an air of modesty. She was feeling more intrigued than irked now.

Well, he was a friendly fellow, at any rate, apparently one with an altruistic streak. But why did he happen to have the sort of equipment she'd normally associate with a phone repairman—or a CIA agent?

Steven was off the phone in a moment, and Justin returned the boy's harmonica. He shook the child's hand, then that of the mother, as the crowd began to disperse.

". . . simple, really," he was saying to the woman. "The computer converts the harmonica's frequencies into the tones of a touch-tone phone. You see, those tones activate the system on certain preset wave-lengths . . ."

His voice was rich, with a pleasingly mellow timbre and an accent she pegged as East Coast. She didn't quite understand him—and she was sure nobody else within earshot did, either—but something about the sound of him touched a chord within her, and she found her eyes riveted to his face as the words washed over her.

". . . and you wouldn't need a dial at all," he was saying. "Of course, they'll never do it," Justin said, winding down. "Too expensive, at least in this decade. But it's a thought."

A thought? It had sounded more like a chapter from a physics text. Lydie shook her head. A brain like that didn't often come in a package like his. Just who *was* Justin Fuller, anyway?

On closer inspection, she could see more character in that handsome face. His skin shone with vitality, but had yet to see the sun this summer. A little network of lines around his eyes indicated he was far from carefree, and the eyes themselves had emotion in them. And experience—perhaps more than his youthful appearance suggested.

She knew instinctively that a battery of women

before her had felt the same impulse—to brush that lock of hair off his forehead—and she stifled it. She was inspecting the upward curve of his lips, intrigued by their sensual promise, when she realized he had caught her in midperusal. Once more the eyes gleamed at her. There went her pulse again. Lydie moved forward as he bent down to recoil his wires from the telephone receiver.

"Mr. Fuller?"

He straightened, and Lydie suddenly felt as if she were looking up a couple of feet into those green-brown depths. Would you call them hazel? "Yes?" He was looking at her with undisguised interest.

"I'm your taxi," she said.

"You?" An eyebrow rose.

Lydie took a step back, apprehensive suddenly. Anyone with eyes that sensual and a build that good should have an ego big as Lake Michigan.

For a moment his dark eyes appraised her. She steeled herself for the come-on line that seemed imminent. But he merely nodded.

"Well, mission accomplished," he muttered.

"That was quite a show," she said.

Justin shrugged. "I'm lucky the raw materials were at hand," he said, waving a good-bye to the boy and his mother, who were now exiting. "Otherwise we all might have been stranded for a while."

"Nice of you to help out."

Justin made a little grimace. "Well, once I had it set up . . ." He shook his head. "The things a guy has to do to call himself a cab around here."

True humility? Or . . . Lydie detected a note of serious annoyance. "Well, it's nobody's fault, really—"

"First I find out that every rental car in town's been taken by a Shriner—no, I'll handle this one—"

His firm grip on her wrist had stopped Lydie from lifting the computer case. Skin tingling, and pulse suddenly risen sharply, she lifted the other case and fell into step with Justin as he strode toward the terminal doors.

"—and then I find the only public phone for miles has its touch-tone dial crowbarred. Is that what people do for kicks around here? Deface and destroy?"

"No," Lydie began, startled by his evident irritation. He was turning from Good Samaritan to Mr. Cranky right before her eyes, like some sort of Jekyll and Hyde. "What do you—"

"Hicksville," Justin muttered under his breath, pushing the door open for her. "So where's the cab?"

He was squinting in the sunlight. Lydie gazed at him evenly. "You're looking at it," she informed him.

Justin regarded the Volvo. "That's a cab?"

"It'll get you there," she said sharply, her own irritation rising to keep up with his. "Look, if you'd rather walk from here to Birchwood, I'm sure we can arrange—"

"No, no, it's fine," he interrupted, with an impatient wave of his hand. He reached for the door, then started back as Scruff's head suddenly appeared in the window, teeth bared and growling. "Who's your friend?" he asked Lydie.

Lydie stifled a smile. "His name's Scruff," she said. "And he's usually quite friendly to strangers. Unlike some," she added pointedly.

Justin turned to face her, and his scowl slowly gave way to a sheepish expression she found oddly endearing. "Sorry," he said gruffly. "It's been a long . . .

week," he finished. "Your cab is quite lovely and so is your dog. You're lovely, too," he added, that mischievous twinkle glimmering in his dark eyes. "What's *your* name?"

"Lydie Henley," she told him warily. The man was a regular chameleon.

"Lovely name," he said. "First base? Center?"

Startled, she stared up at him, then realized he was referring to her baseball cap. "Left field," she murmured. She couldn't quite decide if he was mocking her or not. He was extending his hand. She put out her own.

Justin shook it. His grip was firm and warm, setting off a series of unaccountably stimulating sensations inside of her. Her palm tingled, arm shivered, and insides trembled. This was not the reaction the everyday handshake elicited from Lydie Henley. There was something about Justin Fuller's physical presence that made her think she needed a cold shower, quick.

Lydie disengaged her hand and walked swiftly around the car. Drive, she told her body, that's all that's required of you, thanks; we could do without the earth-moving shivers and shakes just now. She got into the car, aware that Justin was sharing the front seat and vaguely annoyed with herself for thinking anything of it. Disgruntled, she took off her cap and shook out her hair.

As she pulled away from the curb, Scruff settled his head on the top of the seat in between them, and Justin gave him a friendly pat. "What's wrong with his leg?" he asked.

"He broke it on a wild-chipmunk chase at the start of the summer," Lydie told him. "Scruff's never been the best hunting dog. In Birchwood he's known as the un-retriever."

Justin chuckled. "Birchwood? That's where I'm headed. Do you know the town? Is it far?"

"I know it, all right," she said dryly, turning back onto Route 22. "I live there."

"Oh," he said. The pleased surprise in that one syllable was a little unsettling.

"In fact, you're staying at my place—I mean, my parents' place," she corrected quickly as one of his bushy black eyebrows shot up. "The Henleys' cabin."

"You're them? I mean—" He stopped himself. "Lydie Henley. Right. What a coincidence." Though her eyes were on the road, she could feel his gaze exploring her features. "Or is it fate?" he added, with a husky undertone in his voice she found vaguely disconcerting.

"Not really." She shrugged. From Mr. Hyde to Romeo. What next? "I drive a cab here a few days a week, and there's only two of them in Traverse City, one airport, and one flight on Sundays. So..."

"I see," Justin murmured, and he let out a deep sigh. "So here I am: nowhere. And Birchwood— that's one gas station and one general store and one restaurant, I guess. Is there more than one good-looking cabdriver? Or do you have that particular slot sewn up?"

Lydie shot him a withering glance. She didn't like his attitude or his backhanded compliments. "You're not particularly impressed with northern Michigan so far, I see," she said stiffly. "What brings you out here?"

Justin pursed his lips and gazed moodily through

the windshield. "I was forced into it," he said at length.

"Forced?" Her Lake Leelanau chauvinism rose to the bait. "It's a beautiful piece of country," she said. "You could do a lot worse."

"I'm sure I could," he said. "It just wasn't my idea to come out here."

"Then whose was it?"

"A well-meaning friend," he said ruefully, and was silent.

"Oh," she said, disconcerted by this sudden mysteriousness. As the silence continued, her feelings of defensiveness about the lake peninsula continued to simmer. "Perhaps you'll be lucky, then," she found herself saying, "and your stay will be very short."

He gave her a look that instantly communicated he was taken aback by her rudeness. Lydie felt a flush of embarrassment. But his gaze lingered on her nose, lips, chin, seeming to assess the softness of her skin, and she felt the flush suffuse her body, traveling to deeper regions. Lydie forced her eyes to mind the road.

"I'm sorry," he said at length. "This looks like a really wonderful piece of country, really..."

"It is," she said grimly, peering through the windshield. There was a large fruit truck ahead of her making a rather precarious turn. She downshifted.

"...but to tell you the truth, I would think anybody with half a brain would go crazy here within a week."

Lydie saw red. It didn't matter that a small voice in her head was reminding her that those had been her exact sentiments when she'd first returned, not so long ago.

"Look, Mr. Fuller," she said icily. "You may be used to sophistication and nonstop excitement in whatever city you come from, but I can assure you that Birchwood, or any other small town in these parts, doesn't lack for intelligence, or stimulation, or entertainment— Damn!"

Abruptly, she slammed on the brakes. The Volvo shuddered. Screeched. Scruff howled, and Justin Fuller's arm was suddenly pinning her back to her seat.

The fruit truck hadn't made the turn. The load it was dragging had been upended, and the road was now a gleaming sea of red cherries. A few splattered on the windshield like little crimson bombs. The car slid and jerked to a stop.

Lydie's heart pounded like a jackhammer in her chest. She looked down at Justin's warm and muscular arm resting against her, just beneath her breasts, sending hot rushes of tingling sensation coursing through her body. Clearing her throat, Lydie removed the arm.

Justin Fuller surveyed the masses of cherries that surrounded them on all sides and turned to Lydie, his face a picture of implacability. "You're absolutely right," he said in a laconic drawl. "I haven't had this much excitement in years."

CHAPTER TWO

"THIS IS IT?"

Lydie gave Justin a wary look as she shut the motor off. They had just pulled up outside the lake cabin, and he was gazing at it with something like disbelief in his eyes.

"This is it," she told him, ready to do battle at this point.

After she had extricated them from the river of cherries on Route 22, conversation had dwindled to a bare minimum. But she could sense Justin Fuller's continued dissatisfaction with what he obviously considered one of the furthest reaches of modern civilization.

If he made one more critical comment about the lake area or anything in it, she'd take his magical computer and put it—

"Nice piece of property."

Really? Nice of him to say so. To Lydie's eyes, the lakeside cabin and the woods around it were a few acres of country paradise. The cabin was a simple, squat building of wood and stone. But it had been in the family since it was first constructed, and it bore the traces of many a Henley's love and care.

The steps, for example. She remembered when she was a little girl, watching Grandpa saw each plank of wood and painstakingly set the cement for a less steeply graded entrance to the cabin. She could remember Aunt Helen making new curtains for the windows.

Lydie herself had contributed bookshelves to the main room and a little garden area out back. The lilacs that she'd planted when she was a teenager still flourished, growing wild along the path.

"This belongs to your family? All of it?"

Lydie nodded. "The dock's ours, too. There's a boat and some rafts down there."

Justin followed her gaze to the shimmering line of lake visible through white birches. Scruff had managed to bolt through the open car window. He was loping around the dock now, chasing sparrows at the water's edge. A family of birds lived in the eaves of the small boat shed there. They loved to dive-bomb Lydie when she got the rowboat out, and to tease Scruff with low-flying aerial displays.

Lydie couldn't contain a little sigh of regret. No more boating excursions for her this summer. Unless she got an invitation from Mr. Nature, here.

Justin was surveying the lake and land with an expression she couldn't fathom—something between pleasure and vague confusion. Had he grown up with pavement beneath his feet, and never even seen the great outdoors?

"I smell..." He was wrinkling his nose.

"Apples," she told him. "Those are fruit trees over there."

The cabin was surrounded by white pines, some birch, and some gnarled apple trees on the edges of the property. The nearest cabin was invisible through the greenery, so there was a sense of real seclusion and privacy. If that was what one wanted, she couldn't think of a better place to go for it.

Justin Fuller, on the other hand, didn't seem a good candidate for quiet and relaxation. He'd climbed out of the car and was pacing around the dirt driveway.

"It does have electricity?"

Lydie considered saying he'd need candles—and sticks to rub together to make fire—but she controlled herself. "Yes, it does," she assured him, starting up the path. "And hot and cold running water, with strong water pressure, and a couple of heaters, and a telephone."

She paused at the top step, getting the key out of her jeans pocket, a sudden jolt of panic taking hold. Good grief—she'd forgotten completely what a mess still lay within. Not expecting Justin for another eighteen hours, she'd left bits of her . . . everything. All over the place.

"We thought you were coming tomorrow," she said, her hand hovering over the doorknob. "I've been using the cabin myself, and I haven't had a chance to really . . . clean up."

Justin, poised on the step behind her, gave a shrug. "That's all right," he said. "I guess I should've phoned ahead. But you see, I nearly didn't make it up here at all, and at the last minute . . ."

His voice trailed off as he stepped into the cabin behind her. Lydie, without even pausing in her stride, made a beeline for the open drawers of the pine dresser. She'd been looking for a favorite old T-shirt of hers in there that morning, and of course, half of all the clothing she owned was now strewn in piles at the foot of the chest.

"You were saying?" Keep him talking. Maybe that way he wouldn't notice the utter disarray. The kitchen, she noticed with a panicked glance, looked like a disaster area.

"Well, I had made other plans," he went on, putting his suitcase down by the table in the main room. "Then Handleman intercepted me and practically forklifted me into an airplane."

"Handleman?" Her bag seemed to have shrunk since her arrival—either that, or she'd somehow acquired twice as many clothes since. How was she supposed to get all of this out of here in one trip?

"Luke Handleman." Justin's footsteps were headed for the little bedroom. She heard him pause at the half-open door and jiggle the knob. "He's my . . . well, he calls himself my keeper. He's the guy who asked Pete Koska about this place."

So Justin Fuller needed a keeper? Somehow not surprising, even though she couldn't imagine what he needed to be kept from doing. Disassembling the nationwide telephone system whenever he had to wait for taxicabs?

"I think this must be yours."

Lydie turned around. Justin was holding a bra in his hands, and his eyes seemed to be exploring its dimensions with interest. Feeling crimson heat seep into her cheeks, Lydie quickly took it from him. Why she'd chosen to hang that particular article of clothing from the bedroom doorknob was beyond her, but she surely wished she hadn't.

"Sorry," she mumbled, stuffing it into her bag.

Justin's eyes were glimmering with a light she didn't like the looks of. Clearing her throat, she quickly turned her back to him again, suddenly as self-conscious as a junior high school student. We're adults, she told herself, checking the cedar chest for any other surprises. It wasn't *you* the man had in his hands, it was only—

A sudden clatter behind her made her whip around, the bag overflowing with clothes in her hand. Justin Fuller had tripped over her rod and reel, which for some reason she'd left leaning against the kitchen table. She didn't know whether to wince or grin as he caught his balance by grabbing on to the kitchen counter, a befuddled expression on his face.

"Yours?" He was indicating the tangle of line under the table.

Lydie nodded. "Sorry about that," she said pleasantly. "Do you fish?"

This seemed to amuse Justin. A smile stole over the features that had darkened when he stumbled, this smile a little lazier and slow. "No," he said. "Is that what people do out here?"

"Some," she said. "The fudgies—" She stopped, about to blush again in earnest.

"The what?"

"Fudgies," she sighed. "That's what we call the summer people. You see, there's a lot of homemade fudge sold at the shops in the harbor, and invariably—"

"Got it," he said. "Do go on."

"Well, the summer people come up here to fish, mainly. There's a lot of boating, and some hunting . . ." Her voice trailed off. He was watching her again, with a mischievous gleam in his eye. She cleared her throat. "And what do *you* have in mind?"

She'd no sooner said it than she regretted the all-too-easily misinterpreted question. Talk about a setup, she thought with an inward cringe.

But Justin, remarkably, merely shrugged, looking away from her to study the windows behind her. "I haven't the slightest idea," he said quietly in a musing tone that was tinged with honest wonder.

Did the man thrive on being cryptic? He was turning into a full-fledged enigma. Lydie had never been very patient with enigmas, especially ones with bedroom eyes and slightly schizophrenic tendencies.

That was the thing about Justin Fuller, she realized: She couldn't pin him down. Which man was he really? The nice, fatherly fellow who'd entertained a young boy with harmonica and computer? The citified snob who'd been disparaging her hometown? Or the almost too-attractive specimen of masculinity who kept making her pulse rise when he looked at her?

Even that last aspect was confusing. His eyes had held unmistakable interest, but he wasn't being at all aggressive.

It didn't add up. Lydie was trying to formulate another question that wouldn't seem too nosy, when Justin broke the silence. "It's pretty," he allowed, surveying the greenery that beckoned beyond the white curtains. "What happens here in the winter?"

"Nothing," she told him wryly. "The lakes freeze over and the people make like bears."

"You, too?"

Disbelief was evident in his voice. "Well, no," Lydie allowed, wondering what it was about *her* appearance in particular that suggested she wasn't the hibernating type. She nervously fingered the top button of her man-tailored shirt, wondering why she had chosen this particular day to go braless. Though she wished it wouldn't, the thin cotton was sticking to her skin. "I mean, I haven't been here in the winter for years. But when I lived here before—"

"Where have you been?"

"East," she said. Two could play at being cagey.

"Manhattan?"

She nodded. "Seven years in the big city."

"So you're back for the summer? Visiting your folks?"

"That's right." It was a white lie, but it would do. She didn't see any need to share her personal problems with Justin Fuller. "And where are you...coming from?" she asked, still interested in trying to combat his inquisitiveness with some of her own.

"West," he said. And clammed up. Abruptly, he turned away, bending down to remove a power cord from his computer case.

All right, be that way, she fumed. Then she steadied herself. Just because she was naturally gregarious, used to getting to know people quickly and happy to have them know her, didn't mean he had to be. And why should she care?

He was searching for an outlet now. Lydie, watching him, was taken with a peculiar thought. Was Justin Fuller possibly...shy?

For someone so erudite, he did seem at a loss for words. She stole another glance at him, and he met her eyes. Then he smiled, inexplicably upping her pulse rate once again, and Lydie decided she'd figured him wrong. No one with magic eyes and a grin that sexy could be bashful.

Now Lydie was the one to turn away. Her eyes

roved over the interior of the cabin's main room. What else needed collecting? She stepped past Justin to the bedroom. Good Lord. Makeup, sketchpads, mail—the bed. She would put fresh sheets on.

She heard a muttered curse behind her and spun around. What now?

"You don't have any three-prongs," he said darkly.

"Excuse me?"

"Outlets, three-prong outlets. When was this cabin built, anyway?"

"Sixty years ago. Prior to three-prongs, I guess," she said dryly. "Maybe you'd rather move into a motel."

Justin met her challenging thrust of chin with a sudden flash of humor in his eyes. "You'd like that, wouldn't you?"

Lydie shrugged. "You're the one being inconvenienced."

"Well, it's just that my computer needs a certain kind of socket . . . but there must be a decent hardware store in town where I can get an adapter."

Lydie said nothing for a moment, enjoying the look of anxious apprehension that flickered across his features. "Yes, there's a good one," she assured him then. "Are you and that thing attached at the hip, or something?"

Justin chuckled. The warmth in the husky timbre of the sound surprised her. "No," he said, with a rueful grin. "But I do need to use it."

"Aren't you on vacation?"

His smile faded. The word didn't seem to sit well with him. "Exile is more like it," he muttered. "Hmm. I think I took a battery pack along . . ."

As he knelt down, opening up his other suitcase,

Lydie returned to the bedroom. She ripped the sheets off the bed with a little more force than necessary. Had *she* been like that when she'd first returned? All wired up and impatient? No wonder people had given her a wide berth for those initial few days. Well, she'd be happy to leave him stewing in his own circuits—as soon as the bed was made.

She got clean sheets from the cupboard, and was unfolding the top one when Justin appeared in the doorway.

"Are you in your blue period?"

It took her a moment, but then she saw the smudge of aquamarine around his thumb tip and forefinger. Oh, damn—that experiment with oil-base paint she'd worked on in the morning hadn't dried yet. The little canvas was propped up by the kitchen sink, along with her brushes and the tubes.

"Not really," she said. "I mean, it's not a blue period, so to speak." He was looking at her with undisguised curiosity, in a way that made her feel a bit like a rare bird. Disconcerted, she fumbled for an explanation, wondered why she felt she needed to explain herself, and gave up. "I've been dabbling with oils lately—"

"When you're not in the library," he ruminated. "Studying up on the Impressionists."

She shot him a startled look. "All right, Sherlock—"

"One of them's overdue," he said, gesturing toward the pile of books she now remembered were on the floor behind him. "How are the nasturtiums?"

That was one guess that was too good. There wasn't anything in the cabin that could have suggested her last trip to Peplinski's nursery—except the empty seed packages she now noticed right under Justin's feet. Lydie smiled. "Fine, thanks," she said. "And yours?"

"I don't have any," he said. "I have what you'd call a black thumb. Plants die on me almost immediately after contact."

This was his most personal admission thus far, so she supposed she should have been pleased. But it irked her, realizing he was soaking up all the details of her personal life while he remained inscrutable. "I'll be out of your way in two minutes," she said. "And I'll sweep up as soon as the bed's made."

"Let me give you a hand."

"No, that's okay—"

Too late. He'd already grabbed the other corner of the top sheet. Lydie stepped back, focusing her attention on spreading the sheet out. She could feel his penetrating glance sweep over her features again.

"So you're a painter?"

"No." The answer was out of her mouth with automatic, reflexive vehemence.

"But you're excellent."

Lydie looked up to meet his eyes across the bed. The sheet was taut in her hands. Whether he realized it or not, Justin was entering an extremely sensitive area—an invisible little minefield with Keep Out signs posted at all borders. "Not really," she demurred.

"Yes, really," he insisted, holding her gaze. "Why the false modesty?"

Lydie pulled the sheet toward her, and Justin gave a little lurch, nearly losing his balance. "It's not modesty," she said through tightened lips, as she tucked in a corner. What did he know about art, anyway?

"Your color sense is extraordinary," he said, tucking in his corner. "And the foreground-background relationship you've got going there is unusually complex. Are you familiar with Rick Klauber's work?"

Lydie looked up at him, startled. Klauber, not well known by the public at large, more an "artist's artist," had been a major influence on her painting . . . when she had been painting in earnest, years ago. "I know it well," she allowed. "How do you—"

"I bought one of his smaller canvases in New York, the last time I was in town," said Justin. "Have you had exhibits there?"

One of the imaginary mines exploded. She could feel the detonation in her stomach. Lydie turned from the bed as her face fell. She rummaged in the cupboard for Grandmother's old quilt. "Are you kidding? Getting into a gallery in Manhattan with my stuff is like trying to climb Mount Everest in sneakers."

"I see," Justin murmured.

Lydie turned back to the bed, quilt in hand. What did he mean by that: He saw? What did he see?

"You mean you've given up," he said quietly.

What was he trying to do, blow himself sky-high? Hadn't he seen the signs? "No, I just branched out," she said, dangerously calm.

"Into what?" Eyes never leaving her face, he took an edge of the quilt in hand.

"Graphics. I've been working as an art director. At *Eighteen* magazine."

"Really? That's a shame."

There was something accusatory in his voice that was very irritating. She was allowed to be judgmental, hard on herself, sure—but who was he? "Some of us like to eat, you know," she said acidly.

"But how can you waste your talents?" he asked.

Lydie stared at him, unable to keep down the outrage that was mingling with other pent-up feelings, suddenly uncorked. "Look, Mr. Fuller—"

"Justin."

"—you've done nothing but offer your unasked-for opinions ever since you arrived here. You've been criticizing everything you see, but—"

"Lydie . . ."

"—I'd appreciate it if you didn't criticize *me*."

"Hold still," he murmured.

"What?"

As she glared at him, uncomprehending, he reached across the bed. His face was suddenly quite close to hers; his fingers brushed her hair. Startled, she stared at him, then looked down to see the furry strip of green on his forefinger.

"Someone about to visit your left ear," Justin said softly, a faint smile turning up the edges of his mouth.

Lydie bent forward, her anger arrested as she looked at the beautiful, tiny thing. The caterpillar was all fuzzy stripes and wiggles, turning about on Justin's finger in confusion.

"Didn't mean to disturb you," Justin murmured, seeming to address the agitated creature. But Lydie sensed the apology hovering behind those playful words. She couldn't keep a smile from tugging at her own mouth.

When she looked up, his eyes seemed perilously close, their dark velvet depths glimmering with gold flecks of inviting warmth. She felt a little tremor go through her as he held her gaze, and she parted her lips, about to say something, though she didn't know what.

But then, inexplicably, Justin's lips were swooping down to claim hers. Her breath caught in her throat at the shock of warm, soft skin against hers.

She was suddenly engulfed by confusing sensations—a liquid warmth spreading like heated honey from her mouth to the rest of her now-trembling body; a clean, musky male scent filling her nostrils; a rising thunder in her chest that she dimly realized was her pounding heart.

He was molding her lips to fit his own, his arrogant tongue stealing the moistness from her mouth, probing where it shouldn't probe. Her eyelashes had fluttered closed for no good reason she could think of, and that was the problem—she couldn't think, period.

All she could do was savor the unexpected sweetness of his kiss, and revel in the shiver-inducing exploration of the warm, wet tongue that was finding hers. Her mouth parted wider, her lips matching his gentle pressure with an urgency of her own.

Madness, whispered a little voice. Yes, she answered silently, feeling his hand gently cup her chin, his fingers finding the beating pulse beneath the tingling skin of her neck. But it's certainly an interesting kind of insanity, isn't it?

She'd never known a kiss to be so . . . so *much* of a voluptuously arousing thing. It was as if the very core of her were being urged upward to meet the penetrating heat of him. His lips were coaxing forth a wildness in her blood she'd never known was there.

A sound—half inarticulate murmur, half moan—caught in her throat as her tongue meshed with his in a sensual little dance of inflamed arousal. Her own hands, with a will of their own, were settling on his shoulders as she leaned across the bed, feeling as if she were falling further and further into a spiraling caldron of desire. . . .

A beeping sounded somewhere near her ear. The fingers that had been tenderly playing with the soft tendrils of her hair paused suddenly. And then the lips that had so captivated hers was gone.

She found herself staring into the depths of Justin's eyes, eyes that seemed to mirror her own dazed arousal. "I'm sorry," he murmured.

Sorry for kissing her? Or sorry for stopping? Lydie cleared her throat. She tried to find her voice, which had disappeared. Justin's fingers brushed her cheek as he pulled away, the beeping sound piercing the silence again.

"Have to make a phone call," he muttered, straightening. Lydie's hands slid from his shoulders. She stood up as well, sanity seeping back into her consciousness, and with it acute embarrassment. What in the world had gotten into her?

A blush suffused her cheeks as she silently answered her own question. *He*—that strange, irksome hunk of dangerously alluring masculinity who was backing out of the bedroom now, a peculiarly befuddled expression on his face. Was it her imagination, or was he as taken aback as she was by this sudden turn of events?

Not highly likely. A man who generated erotic wattage like that had to be an experienced and manipulative seducer. At the moment, however, he was bumping into the doorframe, then turning around, disoriented, as the beeper on his wristwatch sounded off again. Lydie had to admit he didn't particularly resemble a practiced playboy.

"Sorry," he muttered. "I didn't mean to . . . Excuse me."

Curiouser and curiouser. Justin vanished through

the doorway. Suddenly alone, she gazed at the quilt their hands had abandoned, feeling as though she'd just stepped off a mini roller coaster ride.

A minute ago she'd been venting her spleen defensively at an insufferably opinionated fudgie who'd barged into her life uninvited. And then . . . Lydie shook her head. Maybe she wasn't herself yet after all. How else to account for her willing surrender to that— Who *was* he, for God's sake?

She could hear Justin's voice in the other room. After quickly straightening out the quilt, she made a hasty survey of the bedroom area. Then, gathering up whatever she could that belonged to her, she hurried through the door.

"Five million?" Justin was saying. He was pacing a circle with a four-foot radius, the phone cord already a helpless tangle. Strange fellow, she mused distractedly. Easy to agitate. But he appeared to have forgotten her completely. Lydie shook her head, wondering if she had dreamed that kiss. But no, her heart was still racing. She'd better pack up her paints . . .

"You know they could do it for less." He sounded disgruntled. "Look, redesign the capacitors in the switchboard; that's the only corner we can reasonably cut. Call Tom at RCV . . ."

With tubes of paint jammed in a paper bag with her brushes and thinner, Lydie took a hasty look around. Well, she had the bulk of it. If she had to come back, she'd—well, whatever. At the moment, all she could think about was leaving, fast.

She strode to the door, managed to get it open with all hands full, and cleared her throat. Justin ignored her. "Ridiculous," he was saying. "If I was there, he'd never—" He seemed about to pace a ring into the pinewood floor. "Well, if I wasn't stuck in this god-forsaken hick town—"

She'd been about to bid him a polite good-bye, at least, though why she felt a need to be polite to someone who'd just kissed her socks off and then summarily abandoned her, she wasn't sure. But his last remark brought to the fore all the reasons she'd initially disliked Justin Fuller.

Without a word, she exited the cabin, letting the screen door slam, and headed for the car. In record time, she'd loaded in her stuff and retrieved Scruff; she was in the driver's seat, turning on the motor, when the cabin door opened again.

"Lydie?" Justin Fuller peered out. "I'm sorry I— hey, what are you doing?"

Ignoring him as he'd ignored her, Lydie shifted gears and pulled down the driveway in a little shower of dirt and gravel. She could hear him calling her name again, but she didn't glance in the rearview mirror.

Later for you, stranger, she thought—but that sentiment had its disturbing connotations. Later? Lydie frowned, driving back to the main road. Yes, there would be a later, no doubt. Birchwood was a small town.

Well, she'd just have to see to it that later was as late as it could be.

CHAPTER THREE

LYDIE PAUSED AT the foot of the steps outside the Henley household, a bag in each hand. Scruff was nudging at the screen door, tail wagging, but Lydie wasn't so impatient to go inside. Was she ready for this?

Being in the cabin was one thing—it had often served as a refuge from the world at large at odd times throughout her childhood—but being under the same roof with the Henley clan was an unsettling prospect. After she'd made such a big deal about flying the coop seven years back...

Well, ready or not, she had nowhere else to go. With a little sigh, Lydie opened the door and stepped into the foyer. A flurry of feathers in her face nearly made her drop her bags. Scruff was leaping in the air, and then gone, barking.

She had a brief glimpse of the white cockatoo zigzagging away from her, followed by the dog, and then muffled thumps and crashes from the direction of the kitchen. She heard her mother chastising the dog and

opening the back door. Aunt Helen appeared at the top of the stairs.

"Lydie? Did you let Scruff in?"

"I'm sorry, Helen, I forgot—but Mom's already got him out of the house."

"Thank goodness . . ." Tongue clucking, the gray-haired woman in a floral housedress descended the stairs, Hilary, the red parrot, perched on her shoulder. "Poor Henry must be frightened silly. Henry?"

Lydie stepped aside as her aunt hurried off calling for her cockatoo. Then Lydie took a peek into the living room through the doorway and paused. Dad and Perry Dunklow were standing at the other end of the room, Perry with a fishing rod in hand, ready to cast.

" 'Scuse me," Lydie said. "I was just—"

"Hi, honey," her father boomed. "Perry's showing me the way some fool up at the lodge went after a smallmouth bass last week."

"Watch this." Perry's wizened face lit up in a grin as he held the rod over his head, pretending to wind up like a pitcher about to throw a ball. Then, with an exaggeratedly wobbly throw, he cast his line to the left of Lydie, hooking the edge of the fringe lamp in the corner.

"Good form," her father chuckled. "What's in the bags, sweetheart?"

"My stuff," Lydie murmured. "Think I'll say hi to Mom."

"Get a taste of that deep-dish cherry pie while you're at it."

Lydie nodded, turned, and set one of her bags down at the foot of the stairs; she was debating whether to put the other in the spare room, when there was a muffled explosion from the attic.

"Gramps?"

Her mother and father's voices rose in unison from opposite ends of the house. After a moment, a door opened above her. "Everything's fine!" Grandpa called, his hearty baritone an assurance that nothing had gone seriously awry. "Just sorting out some Fourth of July leftovers. Don't mind me."

Lydie shook her head, put the other bag down, and walked through the little dining room, following her nose. Mom was at the counter, apron on, hair up, and hands white with dough. A delicious symphony of mouth-watering smells filled the air.

"Hey, Mom."

Mrs. Henley turned, a smile lighting her face. "Lydia! You've come for dinner?"

Lydie shook her head, giving her mother's shoulder an affectionate squeeze as she leaned over to get a look at the latest confections—one fresh out of the oven and another being readied to go in. The pies looked like something out of a bakery window—which made sense, as it was her mother's products that usually filled the display case at Chasen's on River Street in town.

"Let me cut you a slice, dear."

Cherries only conjured up the incident on Route 22, and a certain face she was trying to put right out of her mind. "No thanks, Mom. Any objections to my moving in a day early?"

"None at all, sweetheart. You miss us that much?"

Lydie smiled at the knowing twinkle in her mother's eye. "That guy who rented the cabin showed up early. He's already here."

"Really?" Mrs. Henley bent to trim the edge of her

crust with an artist's attention to detail. "He might've called."

"Yes, but he didn't," Lydie said moodily. "I picked him up at the airport just a few hours ago."

"What's he like?"

Good question. Words failed her as she tried to come up with a brief description. "I don't know. He doesn't seem too happy to be here, though."

Mrs. Henley made a little grimace at the affront. "Then he must be a fool," she said airily. "Lemonade?"

"Sure. I'll get it," Lydie said quickly, crossing to the fridge. "Say, did Pete Koska happen to mention what it is he does?"

"Who, dear?"

"Justin Fuller—the guy who's renting the cabin."

"I haven't the slightest, dear. You could ask your father."

Lydie nodded, pouring herself some lemonade. Her mother collected glasses in the shapes of all manner of things—cartoon characters, lighthouses, national monuments. This one, a large cowboy boot in beveled glass, had been her personal favorite since childhood.

"He doesn't have a car," Lydie mused, lifting the glass to her lips for a sip.

"Who? That man?"

"Shriners snapped up all the rentals in Traverse City. He's sort of marooned for the moment."

"Maybe he'd like to borrow your brother's old three-speed," Mrs. Henley suggested.

The thought of Justin Fuller on a bicycle seemed somehow comical. "Maybe," she said. "Until he can get a car. I'll mention it to him."

"You're going by there later?"

No way.

Although . . . "I might," she mused, wondering why her mind was changing itself on her. Perhaps she was suffering from a little guilt; she hadn't really meant to abandon the man like that, without giving him the lay of the land. But she hadn't been done with her shift in Traverse City, and Marge would have wondered . . . Lydie frowned. That wasn't the reason she'd lit out of there so fast.

"Hey, Miss Lydia!"

Grandpa was down from the attic, his shirt rumpled beneath suspenders stained with soot and gunpowder. He kissed the air near Lydie's face, holding his hands out to show he was too dirty for a real embrace, and headed for the sink.

"Not that sink, please," Mrs. Henley said. "If you insist on trying to blow yourself up in the house, I'm not having you get that grit all over my utensils. Use the basement."

Grandpa winked at Lydie and exited down the pantry stairs. Lydie finished her lemonade in one long, delicious swallow. She glanced at the old clock over the counter. "I'm just going to put my stuff upstairs," she announced. "But I won't be back until after midnight, so don't wait up."

"Indeed?" Mrs. Henley peered over her glasses at her daughter with a mock-suspicious stare. "Got a hot date?"

"Mom, I'm twenty-eight years old," Lydie reminded her. "I'm a woman of the world. I don't have 'hot dates.'"

"And that's a terrible thing," Mrs. Henley said sadly. "Going down to the White Finch, is that it?"

Lydie nodded. She tended bar at the local restaurant

one night a week, usually Tuesdays, but she was filling in for Pam that weekend. "You know anything
about electrical wiring?"

"What's that?" Grandpa was emerging from the
basement, hands clean, face wet and shiny. "What are
you wiring?"

"I'm not," Lydie said. "But the guy who's renting
the lake cabin needs three-prong outlets for his computer."

"Well, well." Grandpa snapped his suspenders,
drawing up his shoulders with a look of great pride.
"There's nothing to a job like that. Why, I could take
care of it in three minutes flat."

"You could?"

"Certainly I could, child—for a slight fee." He
gave her a sideways look and smile. "Perhaps a six-
pack of Rolling Rock."

"It's bad enough you keep fooling around with
ammunition and fireworks, Dad," Mrs. Henley said
darkly. "Now you're going to electrocute yourself?"

"I know all about this stuff, Elly," Grandpa said.
"My brother-in-law was a plumber."

"Plumber?" Mrs. Henley gave a snort. "What's that
got to do with—"

"*His* partner was an electrician!" Grandpa boomed.
"Did you ever meet Harry Polakowski? Now, there
was a man..."

Lydie drifted out of the kitchen, suddenly feeling
very tired. She loved each and every member of her
family—she really did—but she'd been enjoying the
peace and quiet of the cabin. Peace and quiet were
scarce commodities in this house.

Upstairs, she carried her bags down the hall to the
spare bedroom, which shared a bathroom with Aunt

Helen's room. It was only after she'd gone in, raised the shade, and put the bags down that she realized she wasn't alone.

Rabbits. Two of them stared out at her from under the hanging edge of the bedspread. Another one sat atop the bureau, chewing thoughtfully on a cucumber. From the little scurrying noises she could hear now in the bathroom, Lydie gathered it was a fairly large family.

So, Aunt Helen was expanding her menagerie! Lydie sat down in the rocking chair by the window, unfazed. It could have been much worse—snakes, for example. The thought made her shudder.

Lydie caught sight of herself in the mirror over the bureau. She leaned forward, pushing her bangs out of her eyes. How tired did she look? Her shoulder-length auburn hair was a little bedraggled. Her sunburned skin didn't betray any circles beneath the clear blue eyes—circles that could have been there, considering her insomnia last night.

Sleepless nights were supposed to be a thing of the past. Yet another thing she should have left behind when she left the city: that job—that man. But lately they'd returned, and she wasn't sure why. It was two nights in a row, actually; the first was after she'd stayed up late, breaking out her oil paints for the first time in ages . . .

Shrugging, she subjected her features to critical inspection, passing over the high cheekbones, the small, perfectly straight nose, to focus for some reason on her lips. Did they look . . . different? Pursing them, Lydie suddenly realized she was searching for the imprint of Justin's kiss.

She sat back, chagrined. It didn't show, of course;

what a ridiculous thought. But somehow, just thinking about it made her lips tingle and her insides quake.

So don't think about it, she told herself. With a stubborn thrust of her chin, she swept her hair back from her face. The man was too . . . dangerous to play around with. She'd send Grandpa over with the bicycle and his tool kit. And continue to keep her distance.

What had transpired between herself and Justin was a freak occurrence. She'd never met a man who generated such a powerful, sensuous current, who made her feel so much so fast. But if she had any sense, after having just healed a broken heart . . .

There was no way she'd let it happen again.

CHAPTER FOUR

"LAST CALL, GUYS."

"All right, Lydie—then let's have one more round."

Grabbing a frosted mug, Lydie watched the foam rise beneath the running tap. At twenty to midnight, only a few of the regulars were still drinking at the White Finch. The wooden fans whirred slowly overhead and the jukebox was silent, only the ice machine's hum an audible counterpoint to the occasional raucous laughter from the customers gathered at one end of the bar.

She took the beer down there, came back with a couple of empties, and absently rubbed at the small of her back where a dull ache from five hours' work had taken up residence. In another twenty minutes, Willy would be closing up, and she could head home. At least she didn't have to worry about insomnia tonight.

Lydie wiped beads of perspiration from her brow. One of these years Willy was going to get a new airconditioner. The old one had chosen this particular summer to break down. She poured herself a glass of ice water, then looked up in surprise as the tavern door opened.

Justin Fuller? At the White Finch?

Her surprise turned to dismay as he walked slowly up to the bar, his face registering bewilderment. "Excuse me, miss," he said, easing himself onto a barstool. "But haven't I seen you somewhere before?"

"That's an awfully old line," she said wryly.

"So it *is* you," he said, a lazy smile drifting over his features as his dark eyes caressed her face. "I thought maybe you had a twin sister."

Lydie shook her head, aware that the beating of her pulse had risen perceptibly, and unnerved by the phenomenon.

"I know Birchwood's a small town, but..." He frowned, scratching his ear, a thoughtful look in his eyes. "Are you the mayor, too? The chief of police?"

Lydie sighed. "I work here once a week."

"When you're not driving a cab."

"Among other things."

"Such as?"

Lydie shrugged. "You just missed last call. But I'll bend the rules as a friendly gesture. What's your pleasure?"

"Last call?" Justin looked up at the clock. "Are you serious?"

"As a heart attack," she said dryly. "It's Sunday night—and you're in the middle of Hicksville, remember?"

Justin gave a rueful chuckle. "Look, I didn't mean to offend you regarding this place. I'm having a little difficulty . . . adjusting, that's all."

He sounded earnest enough. And his eyes glowed

with a warmth that was hard to resist. Resist! she reminded herself, and looked away into the space over his shoulder. "No problem," she said. "What are you drinking?"

"Actually, I was hoping for a bite to eat."

"At a quarter to midnight?" She shook her head. "I'm afraid the kitchen's closed."

"Really?" He frowned. "Well, is there any place around here where I could get dinner?"

"Dinner?" she echoed. "You mean you haven't—"

"Well, I was on the phone for a while. And then I had some work. You did leave a yogurt in the refrigerator, but I was hoping for something more substantial."

Lydie stared at him, feeling a sudden jolt of remorse. "Oh, dear," she muttered. "And I left you without a... How did you get here, anyway?" she asked.

"I walked," he said.

It was a good four miles from the cabin to town. "Walked," she repeated weakly.

"It was pleasant, actually. Cleared my head out. Of course, I did start out in the wrong direction—"

"Good grief," she murmured.

"—but some kids on motorcycles set me straight. Friendly people up here."

Lydie nodded dumbly. "Well, they should have told you about the grocery store in Hobbs," she said. "It's not as far from where you—"

"Oh, no," he said. "I was thinking I might be able to look you up here in Birchwood. I was worried about you."

"You were worried... about me?"

"Well, the way you ran out before..." His eyes held hers for a moment, and she felt a little tug within her at the glimmer of concern she saw in his steady gaze. "I shouldn't have...kissed you like that," he said softly. "I know it was crazy. I don't know what came over me. I was looking at your lips, and they just looked so infinitely...kissable."

He shook his head. A warm glow emanated from his dark eyes; it made her knees go weak. Those eyes ought to be X-rated, she thought fuzzily.

"I'm sorry," he was saying. "I don't blame you for being upset."

"Oh, I...no," she murmured.

"And I'm sorry I got caught up in that phone call," he said quietly. "It was something I had to take care of that should've taken only a minute. But it did end up taking longer."

"No big deal," she said. "Really, I'm sorry I left you high and dry. I wasn't thinking."

For a moment, she had a vivid memory of just what had caused her to lose all vestiges of rational thought. A little amused glimmer in his eyes made her think he might be remembering, too.

"And, of course, I owed you the fare," he added. "For the cab ride?"

"Oh!" She looked at him, feeling more and more foolish. "I figured I'd get it from you...later. You must be starved," she said quickly. "Let me see what I can—"

"Don't trouble yourself."

"Nonsense," she said. "I'll just go check inside."

But Joseph had already left for the night. Lydie rummaged around in the kitchen. The simplest, fastest thing she could throw together was a cheese omelet.

She was feeling so contrite for having made the man walk four miles to find a meal, she was happy to cook it herself.

Justin hovered in the kitchen doorway as she began beating the eggs. "Sausage? Onions?"

"Sure, whatever you've got," he said. He watched her hustle around the kitchen, his face thoughtful. "So you're a cabdriver, a bartender, a painter, and a cook. Anything else?"

"That's the basic drift," she said, chopping an onion. "And what about you? If you don't mind my asking."

Justin shrugged. "Well, I teach a little here and there, I run a small computer company, and . . . I make things up."

"Pardon?"

"I'm an inventor," Justin said in a tone so offhand he might as well have admitted to a talent for window washing.

Lydie looked up from her eggs. "Really? That's fantastic. What have you invented?"

"Probably nothing you've ever heard of," he said. "Is that sharp cheddar? Good."

"Try me," she said. "What's the last thing you invented?"

"The Juno 3000," he said, leaning past her to pick up a slice of cheese. "It's actually only a variation on an existent machine—a portable version of the Kurtz 200."

"Which is?"

"A reading machine for the blind."

"You're kidding." She slipped a spatula around the edges of the omelet, deftly lifted one side, and flipped it over. "How does it work?"

"Technology's on the complicated side," he said. "But what you do is put a book on the screen, and the computer reads the page and translates it into spoken words. You listen through headphones."

"Really?" She looked at him with renewed respect. "You came up with that?"

Justin shrugged, looking embarrassed. "I just have the patent on the portable version," he said. "It's really no big deal."

"But that's amazing." She flipped the skillet's contents onto a nearby plate, glad to see that she'd made the move without cracking the omelet.

"No, *that's* amazing," Justin said, indicating the plate. "A perfect omelet."

Lydie smiled. "You haven't tasted it yet."

"I can tell it's perfect. When you're an artist, it gets into everything you do. Isn't that right?"

Lydie looked at him. There was a seriousness beneath the light banter that caught her ear and made her heart beat a little faster. She wasn't used to a man understanding her with the intuitiveness she sensed Justin had.

"Right," she said, making light of it. "And aesthetically speaking, that plate would look better with a table underneath it. So if you'll step this way . . ."

Justin followed her back to the bar. She set a place for him, poured him a beer, and went down to the other end to gently but firmly begin the White Finch regulars' evening exodus. Willy helped her, and Gary gave her a hand cleaning up.

There was no time to talk to Justin while she worked, but she felt him watching her as he ate. It was an unusual feeling, but not unpleasant. It occurred to Lydie that it had been a long time since a man had waited for her to get off work.

By the time he was done, so was she. "I'll give you a lift back," she told him, washing his glass.

"Thanks," Justin said. "One head-clearing walk is enough for one night."

"Right," she muttered, still feeling the pangs of guilt. "This way—I'm parked out back."

She bid Willy and Gary good night, and strode quickly to the Volvo. Justin got in, and they were off, passing the sparkle of harbor lights in the warm darkness.

"This is something," he said suddenly, when they'd reached the road that led out of town. "I feel . . . okay."

Lydie couldn't help smiling at the sense of honest wonder she heard in his voice. "You mean that you've survived my cooking?"

"No, no," he said. "It's just that I have this problem . . ."

"Yes?"

"I don't know how to relax."

"Really?"

"Truly." He gazed out the window, brow furrowed. "That's why Handleman set this thing up with Pete Koska. I'm supposed to give it a try."

"You mean relaxing?"

Justin nodded. "He thinks I'm overworked and overextended, a candidate for burnout. So I'm supposed to take a rest. Like it or not."

Lydie glanced at him. Something told her that despite his low-key description of his work, it had to be extremely taxing. "You like to work," she prompted.

"I don't know how to do anything else," he said with a rueful chuckle. "But you know, I've had an inkling. It came over me when we drove by the harbor just now. I was thinking about what a good omelet that was, and what a beautiful night."

"Yes, it is," she said quietly.

"And for a moment there, I felt it."

Lydie smiled. "It?"

"A good feeling. Like being emptied out and filled up at the same time. Tired but still . . . energized."

"That sounds right," Lydie agreed. With anyone else, she realized, she would have been unable to have this conversation and maintain a straight face. A man who didn't know how to do nothing? But she felt somehow that she understood Justin. The problem was real to him.

"And you know what I think?" he continued.

"No."

"I think it has something to do with . . . you."

Lydie swallowed, keeping her eyes on the road. "Me?"

"I mean, I think you have a handle on this sort of thing," he mused. "You emanate a relaxed sort of energy sometimes . . ."

Well, maybe I used to, before you started looking at me with those hazel eyes of yours. Emanating . . . erotica, she thought, shifting uncomfortably in her seat. "You think so?" she asked.

Justin nodded. "Maybe you could help me out," he said.

"Help you out?"

"Yes, maybe you could show me how to get my mind off my work," he suggested. "I have a feeling you could."

Oh, sure, Lydie thought. Oh, yeah. That was just

what she wanted to do—that, or maybe throw herself over Niagara Falls in a barrel. Whichever came up first.

CHAPTER FIVE

JUSTIN WASN'T ANSWERING her knock. Odd. When they'd made this date the night before, he'd assured her he'd be in all morning. And where would a fish out of water like Justin be, anyway?

Ear to the screen, Lydie thought she could hear an unfamiliar rhythmic clicking from within. The door was unlatched. She opened it and took a tentative step inside. Peering into the dim recesses of the cabin, Lydie realized he was practically right in front of her.

Justin hunched over a glowing computer screen, his back to the door. A pair of headphones was clamped over his ears, and his fingers moved quietly over the keyboard in his lap. She walked up behind him, shaking her head as she took in the rest of the tableau.

A miniature cassette recorder was at his side, atop a pile of manila folders. Papers were strewn about his feet. So were: a clipboard, a number of pencils and pens, some computer-printed spreadsheets, and an undrunk cup of coffee.

Justin was unshaven. His hair was more unkempt

than ever and his clothes were the ones he'd worn yesterday. They looked as though they'd been slept in. Maybe they had.

For a moment, she considered letting herself out quietly and returning home. What business had she disturbing the genius at work? But then she remembered, with vivid clarity, the fervent request he'd made when she dropped him off last night.

"Force me," he'd said, his eyes glowing with sincerity. "If I'm left to my own devices, I won't even see the light of day. If I'm not ready to leave when you get here, drag me out regardless, okay?"

How could any woman resist such an earnest plea? He'd taken her up on her idle suggestion of a rowboat trip on the lake as if it were his ticket to mental health. And watching him now, she could see Justin's point. It was obvious that anything but work was a foreign concept to the poor man.

"Justin," she said quietly. He didn't answer, his eyes glued to the bright green screen. Lydie shrugged. She crossed to the picture window back by the door and pulled the curtains open, flooding the room with sunlight.

"Hey!" Justin straightened up, blinking, and gazed confusedly around him. He looked, she realized with an inner twinge, like a little boy interrupted in some serious toy-soldier deployment.

"If this is your idea of rest and relaxation, you're a hopeless case," Lydie told him, systematically lifting shades from the other windows around the room. "It's noon, by the way. Been to bed yet?"

"Briefly," he muttered, with a sheepish look.

Lydie let up the last shade with a bang. She faced him, arms folded, and nodded toward the window.

"Justin Fuller, the sun. Sun, meet Justin Fuller. I'm not sure the two of you are acquainted. But you'll be getting along famously in no time."

Justin yawned, nodded, and held up his forefinger. "'Scuse me," he muttered. "I'll just put this away."

"You've got two minutes," she said. "Boat's leaving."

"No problem," he said, removing his headphones. His eyes lingered on her a moment as he absently shut off his recorder, his expression undergoing a subtle shift. "Say," he murmured appreciatively. "It's good to be seeing more of you."

Lydie glanced down at her turquoise swimsuit, suddenly self-conscious beneath his interested appraisal. It was the first time she'd worn it. She'd tried it on this morning, on a whim she was now regretting.

The sheer one-piece had been purchased in New York. It was really too risqué for Michigan—cut high on the thighs to reveal tan lines formed by other, more conservative suits. Lydie was glad the towel draped around her neck covered the plunging neckline. Justin's palpable perusal of her curves was causing her skin to flush, the all-too-visible tips of her breasts to stiffen beneath the thin material.

"I'll wait for you outside," she said, dismayed at the pinched sound of her voice issuing from her tightened throat. "I mean, you'll want to change . . ."

"Change? Oh, right. Just give me a minute."

To the sounds of his fingers clicking quickly over the keyboard, Lydie slipped out of the cabin, back into the bright sunlight. Now she was the one to feel disoriented, as she headed for the car to get the extra rod and reel. What was it about Justin Fuller that accelerated her heartbeat and shortened her breath when all he did was . . . look at her?

Walking slowly down the path to the dock, she found herself thinking about Martin Talmey again. *He'd* certainly never affected her the way Justin did, with such an immediate physical intensity. And look at the havoc Martin had wreaked with her heart. Who knew what getting more involved with Justin Fuller might do to her?

You're not involved at all, she reminded herself wryly as she opened the door to the boathouse and a swallow went zooming out of the eaves. So there had been one little—okay, not so little—kiss; that didn't constitute an involvement, did it? No. And as long as she kept her head on straight . . .

The rowboat needed bailing. Lydie pulled it closer and began to scoop out the inch or so of water with a handy pail. This simple physical exertion was somehow comforting.

In a few minutes, the job was done and she felt more relaxed. Cool, calm, and collected, she waited on the dock's edge for Birchwood's newest resident to emerge from his cocoon. She was about to walk back to the cabin, fearing Justin had fallen into his computer, when the cabin door opened and the man himself emerged.

Her newfound self-assurance evaporated when she gazed upon the perfectly formed specimen of manhood who was sauntering down the path to the dock. True, Justin Fuller didn't have the seasoned tan most residents sported, but his skin had a healthy glow. And for a man who apparently spent most of his waking hours seated at a desk, he was in the kind of shape some of the hardiest locals would have envied.

Lydie's gaze took in the muscular arms; the broad,

sinewy shoulders; the brawny chest covered with a sexy down of dark, curly hair; a stomach that was flat and firm, and her own body responded with an inner simmering that dimly shocked her.

Lydie's resolutions of noninvolvement underwent a slippery sea change. Maybe just a . . . physical relationship, she mused dazedly. Not that she'd ever been capable of that sort of thing. But maybe she could try it once—

Get a grip, she commanded herself, appalled at her mind's prurient meanderings. You've been single too long, that's for sure. She rose from the dock to greet him with a carefully neutral smile. Justin wore khaki cutoffs, and a vaguely preoccupied expression that indicated he was still blind to the greenery around him.

"I think this is the first time I've seen you without a machine at your side," she said. "How does it feel?"

"Just fine," he answered. Lydie was once again aware of her own state of undress, and she steeled herself for a reprise of his earlier inspection. But his eyes made only the briefest perusal of her swimsuit, then quickly flicked away as if in embarrassment at his own interest.

That was a relief. Lydie was aware that her body was well proportioned, a gift of nature that no amount of overindulgence seemed to alter. She was used to men perusing her with a much less gentlemanly gaze— not that she enjoyed their unasked-for attentions. But Justin apparently had some sense of propriety.

Why, then, did she feel a tiny pang of disappointment as he gazed past her, his eyes on the boat and the placid lake?

"So there's fish out there?"

Happy to get her mind back to the matter at hand, Lydie nodded. "Well, they don't exactly come when you whistle," she said. "But with a little patience . . ."

"I might as well tell you I've never held a fishing pole in my life," Justin said dubiously.

"I won't hold it against you," she said. "Really, Justin, there's nothing to it."

It wasn't until they were pushing off from the dock, tackle box, towels, bait, and poles between them in the bottom of the boat, that Lydie realized she'd skipped an important step. "Here," she said, handing him a dented tube. "You'd better put on some sun block. This noonday sun'll fry you in no time."

Justin nodded, and applied generous gobs of lotion to his arms, legs, and shoulders. It only seemed natural to lend him a hand when he had trouble covering his back. She tried to ignore the shiver that coursed through her as she ran her hands over his skin, but there was no controlling the acceleration of her heartbeat when Justin took it upon himself to return the favor.

"Here, I might as well . . . ," he murmured, and then his strong, warm hands were gently massaging lotion into her shoulders. Of course, she was already deeply tanned from a summer's worth of sun; she should have told him she didn't really need the sun block. But for some reason, her tongue stayed silent as his fingers moved over her taut shoulders. It felt too good to protest.

Abruptly, the hands that were arousing nerve endings she'd forgotten she possessed were gone. Justin held out the tube of lotion, a slightly abashed expression in his eyes. "Thanks," she murmured. Quickly, she applied lotion to the areas he'd stopped short of exploring. Then they were under way.

"Couldn't be a better day for pure relaxation," she told him as a cool breeze ruffled the surface of the water. "We're headed for that cove behind you," she added, pointing.

Justin had manned the oars. He nodded, then leaned into his rowing, favoring the left side. Lydie tore her eyes from the muscles rippling in his powerful forearms and scanned the shoreline. There were no other boats in the immediate area.

"It's nice out here." His voice, tinged with surprise, broke the silence. Lydie saw his expression of grudging admiration for the clear blue water and the unbroken line of greenery shading the shoreline, and she couldn't suppress a smile. "When are you going back?" he asked.

She stared at him, momentarily confused. "Where?"

"East," he said. "Aren't you just visiting? For the summer?"

"Well, I'm..." She paused, considered evasion, and then decided there was really no reason to avoid the truth. "I don't know," she said, meeting his inquisitive look straight on. "My plans are a little vague."

"What about your job at that magazine?"

"I quit," she admitted.

"Good for you."

This hearty endorsement of an act that most of her friends found self-destructive in the extreme would have been unexpected coming from anyone else. But based on their conversation the day before, she already had an inkling of where Justin stood.

"Easy for you to say," she muttered. "But it's left me in limbo."

"Limbo isn't the worst place to be," said Justin.

"I've done some creative thinking there, myself."

"But you're probably paid for it," she said ruefully. "I'm not."

Justin shrugged. "I've had my share of peanut-butter-and-jelly diets," he said. "While I was trying to figure out what step to take next. Sometimes being up against it all is just the thing to spur you into action—to take risks you wouldn't take if you were feeling too comfortable."

"I wasn't comfortable at all," she mused, skimming the surface of the water with her fingers as they neared the cove.

"You mean, making good money and doing meaningless work?"

"Yes, that's right." She met his gaze directly, feeling a surge of pride that didn't have the usual defensiveness coloring it. "I began to feel that anybody could be doing what I was doing, designing colorful layouts for the latest fashion tips. There wasn't any of *me* in it. And even though Martin kept pushing me to—"

She stopped abruptly. She hadn't intended to mention Martin or *that* whole mess. But Justin's eyes were glimmering with curiosity and something she imagined might be sympathy. "Your editor?" he prompted.

Lydie nodded. "Martin got me my job at the magazine. He trained me and . . . brought me up there, so to speak."

Justin's eyes had narrowed slightly. "Had he seen your other work? Your painting?"

"Oh, one or two things. But when I met Martin, I was already trying to find commercial graphics work. He liked my portfolio, and one thing led to another . . ."

"Such as?"

Lydie was trying to steer some course that might skim the truth without getting in too deep. But from Justin's tone, she gathered he was already formulating some conclusions. "He hired me as a free-lancer at first," she said evenly. "And pretty soon I became a full-time staffer."

"You were in love with him?"

Startled, she stared at him, the water splashing up from her suddenly clenched hand. Was she that transparent? Or was he that quick to read between her words? "We were going out," she admitted.

"So he wooed you away from your first love."

"My . . . you mean the paintings?" She laughed, but it was a forced sound that came out wrong. "No, I don't blame Martin. I'd already gotten the picture, pretty much. My art wasn't going to earn me a living in New York. So, when he gave me a chance . . ." She shrugged. "Look, I even enjoyed it at first."

Justin said nothing, his arms moving back and forth with easy, even strokes. But his eyes gleamed with an understanding of her that seemed to surpass her own. She felt a sudden need to defend herself. "I know what it must sound like," she said. "But I didn't get involved with Martin until long after I was working for him. I never would have—"

"Of course not, Lydie." It sounded like a reproach. "Don't be silly. I can't imagine you as the immoral, do-anything-to-reach-the-top type. I'll bet you fought it every step of the way."

Lydie laughed. This time her mirth was real, erupting spontaneously. "How long have you known me?" she teased. "Two days, or several years?"

Justin shrugged. His grin lit up his features.

"Yes, I fought it," she said, remembering. "And then I got in too deep . . . and got out," she finished abruptly.

The real fight had been trying to keep the relationship going when Martin had seemed more interested in the magazine than in her. When she'd tried to change things by seeing other people, he'd suddenly turned possessive. Their fights were part of what had sent her packing. . . . Lydie decided she'd rather not think about it.

"Say no more," Justin murmured, his eyes showing concern. Suddenly he looked down, startled. Lydie heard the oar hit bottom just as he felt it. They were already too close to shore.

"Sorry," she said. "I haven't been a good navigator. See if you can steer us out a bit. Then we'll stop and bait our hooks."

She was glad of the opportunity to drop a potentially painful subject, and he seemed to sense this, because the questions stopped. Justin maneuvered accordingly, and before long the dripping oars were inside, the boat swaying in the light breeze as Lydie attached a worm to her hook. She wrinkled her nose at the unappetizing task, but Justin took to it with typical male indifference.

Casting was another matter. Lydie prided herself on having picked up her father's near-professional skill, but Justin was a novice. In his first attempts, he nearly lost the rod altogether. After a brief instructional session that left her convulsed with giggles and Justin in good-natured perplexity, he did master the basics.

"Here's the relaxing part," she explained, settling back with her legs stretched out near his. With bunched-up towels as pillows, they faced each other in the gently rocking boat, lines cast out on either side.

"Aren't we supposed to be on the alert?"

Lydie shook her head. "You'll feel it if you get a bite. Then just reel in. But it usually takes a while."

"Amazing," Justin muttered.

"What is?"

"Well, it seems like all this rigamarole and gear are just an excuse to lie back in the sun for a while."

Lydie smiled. "In a way, they are. Think you can handle it?"

"I'll do my best."

She peered over to see if he was kidding, but Justin seemed genuinely uncertain about such enforced leisure. From the look in his eyes as he gazed out over the water, his hand absentmindedly playing with the reel of the pole propped up at his side, she could see immediately that his mind was light years away. He was probably already back in the cabin with his computer.

"Justin," she said softly.

He looked back at her, his face a blank. "Hmm?"

"It's okay, you know. You don't have to be productive every minute of the day."

He smiled. "It's habitual. I was inventing a machine that could hold your rod for you while you did something else, and sound an alert if a fish bit."

"It's already been invented," she told him. "There are stands for poles, and the reels are natural alarm systems. You hear them unwinding if you're within earshot."

"Of course," he mused. "What was he like?"

"He?" Justin's habit of changing subjects almost in midsentence was a little disconcerting, but she was beginning to get the hang of it. "You mean Martin? Well, he was like you in one way."

"Which?"

"He was a workaholic," she said ruefully. "The man was married to his magazine."

"What did that make you? His mistress?"

She shot him a withering look, but couldn't deny that the metaphor was all too apt. "Things worked out fine once I started keeping the same hours he did," she said. "I got as involved with the magazine as I could."

"So you could be close to him."

Lydie nodded, absently pulling in her line. "But after a while it was a losing battle." Especially when she discovered that his vague promises of an eventual marriage were so much smoke.

She didn't want to reactivate those volatile feelings. It had taken enough time and effort to bunch them up into a manageable core of hurt and hostility that she could safely pack away, deep inside of her. Frowning, she reeled in faster, wondering why she'd let herself be this open with a stranger to begin with.

"So you had more than one reason to leave New York," Justin was saying. She was about to give him a curt reply and change the subject, when a tug of her reel made her sit up hurriedly.

"Got one," she murmured. The line was pulling fast and hard. She was trying to keep her balance and continue reeling in what appeared to be a fish of some size, but the boat rocked beneath her.

"Careful," came a husky murmur at her ear. Two strong arms were around her waist, hands clasped gently but firmly over her midriff. She could feel Justin's lanky, muscular body against hers, one leg on either side of her, as she struggled with the rod, and the sensation was so distracting that she nearly let the line go.

"It's okay," she gasped, breathless. "I've got everything under control." Everything except her pounding heartbeat and careening pulse as the disorienting feeling of being held in Justin's arms overpowered her. The pole jerked in her hand, dipping precariously toward the water.

As she leaned forward suddenly, his hands slipped upward, grazing the underside of her breasts. Steam seemed to cloud her vision as his touch raised goose bumps on her skin and her heart invented a new kind of double-time rhythm. The fish was tugging, but she was the one who felt caught.

Arching her back to pull the rod upright, she felt enveloped by the musky male scent of him, the hot feel of his arms enfolding her, the warm breath near her ear as he reached out to steady her arm. She could feel his thighs straining against hers, and the evidence of his own arousal through the thin material.

Something had to give. She chose the fish. Whether it was a conscious move or not, the reel slipped from her firm grip. The line whipped out rapidly, then went slack with a little jerk that probably signified the fish's escape.

"Lost it," she muttered, and he let go of her arm. Lydie turned to face him, aware that his other arm was still sliding around her waist, but she was unable to move away in the confined space.

"Sorry," Justin said, with a sheepish smile. "I was only trying to help."

His face was so close, that curl of soft hair over his eyes so touchable. Her body was trembling for no good reason in his gentle grasp. "I was doing fine," she said. "You didn't really need to..."

Justin nodded. "I know. But I think I needed to hold you," he said quietly, those dark eyes mesmerizing hers, the flecks of gold glimmering invitingly in the velvet depths.

His honest admission only served to make the blood simmer and race in her veins. She was trying to think of a suitable reply, when he brought his lips even closer. "And now that I'm holding you..."

The sentence ended with a kiss that took her breath away. Her face tilted up, and her limbs turned to liquid. Her eyes closed, the lids suddenly too heavy to keep open. As if drugged, she gave herself over to the moist softness of his lips molding to hers.

Justin's tongue probed inside her mouth, finding her tongue, toying with it, eliciting a soft moan from deep inside her. Little sunbursts seemed to go off behind her eyes as, involuntarily, she shifted her body in his embrace, one hand slipping around his neck.

She could feel the taut points of her breasts against the burly softness of his chest, feel his hands spreading a sensuous liquid heat over the small of her back, the curve of her buttocks. She lost herself in the blossoming arousal, the sweet-salty taste of him, the deliciously delirious abandonment she felt as he pulled her even tighter.

She heard the little splash behind her and realized it was her fishing rod. She'd dropped it, her fingers gone slack in the heat of flaring desire. Then Justin's lips left hers, and she opened her eyes to see him looking at her, an expression of surprised delight on his face.

"Hey," he murmured. "You didn't seem to mind that, did you?"

She could only stare at him, momentarily mute, feeling less surprised—but certainly more concerned—than he was. How could she be letting herself—

"Your pole," he muttered, with a sudden frown. He released her and, with the grace of a practiced athlete, dove past her into the clear blue water. As the spray hit her, she turned to watch him, wondering if she was perhaps suffering from sunstroke.

No. It was lust, pure and simple. She'd never believed in chemical combustion between men and women, but she realized now that that was only because she'd never experienced it before. Now that she had, she wasn't sure she liked it. This kind of thing happened fast, apparently, and it could scramble one's brains.

Justin surfaced, hair wet and gleaming, her fishing rod held triumphantly in his hand. He was looking anything but scrambled. "The water's great!" he called. A few strokes brought him up to the rowboat's side, and the pole dropped at her feet with a clatter. "Maybe you'd like to join me."

Lydie considered the suggestion. She could use the cooling off, but even though the lake was huge, she had a foreboding she'd somehow end up in Justin's arms again. The man was dangerous at any range. "Not just now," she told him.

Justin hung on to the side of the boat with one arm, his expression more serious. "You probably think I'm kind of crazy," he said.

"Crazy? Why?"

"Kissing you like that—again," he said, looking abashed.

Maybe Justin Fuller was shier than she'd realized. Strange though that might seem. "I'm the crazy one for letting you," she said.

"Maybe so. Maybe you shouldn't have anything to do with me."

He was probably right, she mused. But why was *he* telling *her?* "I shouldn't?"

He shook his head. "To tell you the truth, me and relationships just don't mix."

The words sounded oddly familar. Lydie realized, chagrined, that this was something she'd said herself, not too long ago. "I didn't realize we were in a relationship," she said.

"We're not," he said hurriedly, looking all the more embarrassed. "But we—" He stopped himself and shook his head. "Lydie, I'm not going to deny that you're a very attractive woman," he said soberly. "And I'm very attracted to you. That's why I . . . let myself get carried away. But I'll try not to let it happen again."

She'd heard her share of lines, come-ons, and original approaches. But Justin Fuller's had to be the most unique. The man had sex appeal coming out of his ears, but he was acting as moral and bashful as a citified Jimmy Stewart. Lydie watched his discomfiture with a mixture of sympathy and faint indignation. Did he have to be quite so apologetic?

"Why?" she found herself asking. "Are you involved with someone else?"

"No," he said quickly. "I tried it once, but it didn't last."

This, at least, was a statement she could relate to, although it was certainly ambiguous. Lydie was tempted to probe further, but the somber look on Justin's face stopped her. She could sense the real pain behind his seemingly flippant words. "I see," she said.

"Look, I think it's great of you to be spending time with me like this," he went on hurriedly. "I don't want to spoil it with any complications."

Nice of you, she thought. Why was he back-pedaling so fast and so hard? "Me neither," she told him.

"Well then," he said, "I'll try to behave." With a smile of pure goodwill, Justin let go of the boat and dove below the surface again. Lydie stared at the rippling water, not knowing what to think at this point.

"But Lydie, you know what?" He was floating on his back now, grinning widely, seemingly serene as he drifted nearby. "It worked!"

"What do you mean?"

"I don't have a thought in my head!" he crowed. "I think I'm actually . . . what was the word? Relaxing!"

"Congratulations," she said dryly.

"You're terrific," he called, paddling away. "I couldn't have done it without you."

CHAPTER SIX

AT TWENTY AFTER nine, Lydie got up from the porch hammock and walked down the steps into the front yard for the umpteenth time. How could she be such a prize chump? What was she doing, waiting for a man who was clearly lost in the ozone? And why had she let him talk her into making another date in the first place?

One of Aunt Helen's many rabbits was sitting under the elm tree, fixing her with a baleful gaze. Lydie sat down in the grass a few yards away, smoothing her dress around her knees. And she'd even worn her white summer shift with the scooped back and lace trim, she reminded herself, for this platonic tryst that was looking less likely to materialize with each passing minute. Her own actions suddenly didn't make sense to her, let alone Justin Fuller's.

After their fishing outing, he'd offered to take her to dinner the following night. Tonight. At the time, it had seemed natural to accept. He was being friendly, making it clear that he wasn't trying to seduce her but was sincerely enjoying her company and was interested in finding out more about Birchwood.

So she'd agreed. Why? Lydie stared up at the stars, trying to remember her rationale while her stomach growled plaintively. Well, she was tired of picking at odds and ends from the refrigerator, and wary of making family dinners a nightly habit. And she'd enjoyed talking to him. Especially the way he'd listened to her—with real interest, asking perceptive questions.

And she'd told herself that the sexual attraction could be ... "handled." They were mature adults. Neither wished to get involved on any serious level. So why should she feel remorse over having agreed to see him again?

So why wasn't he here?

Lydie got up and restlessly paced the yard. He'd rented a car that morning, she knew; she'd heard about it through the lakefront grapevine. News that a computer-carrying intellectual had taken up residence in the Henleys' cabin was already common knowledge.

If he had a car and he had directions, what was the man's problem? With an exasperated sigh, Lydie headed for the house. A phone call from Justin would be only polite, after an hour. Well, she wasn't about to stand on ceremony. She'd call him.

Busy signal.

When the line was still busy on the third try, mild exasperation gave way to simmering anger. She was too old for this sort of thing. She was also caring too much about this casual non-date-date. Which only irked her all the more.

Lydie drove into town and had a burger at the White Finch. She traded quips and friendly insults with Jimmy, the bartender, who pretended to disbelieve

she'd ever been a local girl. They'd struck up a friendship when she started working there at the beginning
of the summer, and he liked to tease her about her
"Big Apple attitude."

"You're looking restless tonight, Lydie." Jimmy
wiped some froth from his mustache as he set his beer
mug on the bar by her place setting. "Bored with the
small-town life so soon?"

"Could be," she admitted. "It's just another long,
hot night."

"True enough," he admitted. "Well, you could drive
around the lake with the windows open and listen to
those raucous rock 'n' roll tapes of yours."

"I've worn 'em out," Lydie told him. "Say, why
is it that Powell's only seem to get in new cassettes
twice a year?"

"There you go again," Jimmy huffed. "I suppose
you had a stereo store right on your corner in New
York? That got in the latest hits on an hourly basis?"
He paused. "And they delivered?"

Lydie laughed. "Sorry, Jim. I didn't mean to slip
back into my critical mode. But you've got to admit
there's a certain lack of excitement around here."

Jimmy raised a bushy eyebrow. "You could wait
for me to get off work."

Lydie smiled. She liked Jimmy, but that was it.
Though this had been understood between the two of
them from their first meeting, he enjoyed indulging
in the occasional harmless flirtation. And feeling as
she did tonight, the attention was welcome.

"Thanks, but no thanks, Jim," she said, then added
with an archly coquettish bat of her eyelashes: "Don't
give up hope, though. What do I owe you?"

The two beers she'd drunk with dinner had taken

some of the edge off, and Lydie was a little more relaxed as she drove home. She slowed down near the turnoff to the cabin and, on an impulse, made the turn. Maybe Justin Fuller could be prevailed upon to provide some good excuse for standing her up.

She parked a ways down the dirt drive and got out, peering through the darkness to see if the lights were on in the cabin. They were. Feeling both devious and righteously justified, she crept quietly down the drive, then moved around the side of the cabin to take one quick glance through the window.

There was Justin Fuller, his face buried in his computer screen, a phone at his ear, and a calculator in his hand.

She might have known. The man was hopeless.

But Justin's obsessive absorption in his work didn't excuse him in her eyes. And it just made her feel all the more foolish. Lydie stifled her temptation to throw a good-sized rock through the cabin window. Instead, she sauntered down to the lake and began to remove her clothes.

Late-night skinny-dips in the lake had been her favorite ritual all summer long. Justin Fuller's unwanted presence had deprived her of two such sessions. Lydie was about to make up for lost time.

She hung the white dress from the bough of a beech that hung out past the dock, deposited her underwear on the lone folding chair at the dock's end, and waded knee-deep into the wonderfully ice-cold water. When it rose to her thighs, she arched her body and dove.

She surfaced from the icy darkness and flipped over onto her back, luxuriating in the feel of water rushing softly around her limbs. The water was a blessed relief after the hot mugginess of the summer night. She swam through the darkness, hair streaming around her face, the whiteness of her skin gleaming in the moonlight. And for a moment, life was good again.

Turning over onto her stomach to face the shore, she saw the lights glimmering from the cabin, and the moment passed. She sighed, swimming into the shallows, and stood, enjoying the feel of the cool water streaming down the curves of her nude body. But her eyes stayed fixed on the cabin.

You don't know what you're missing, Justin Fuller.

Any red-blooded American male would make a mad beeline for the dock if he caught a glimpse of this mermaidlike vision in the lake. But Justin, who assuredly wasn't like any other male she'd ever met, wasn't even sufficiently attuned to the sounds around him to be aware of her presence.

Oh, sure, she didn't care, she thought wryly as she swam off again, doing a lazy backstroke, her eyes fixed on the stars above. She was going to live her single life, detached and uninvolved with no need of male companionship. Right. That had been the plan—up until two days ago.

Then *he'd* turned up.

She'd tried to pretend that the kisses didn't matter, the mind-numbing, body-galvanizing embraces. He didn't want involvement, and neither did she. Simple, right? Lydie turned and dove beneath the surface. She was getting a little tired, and even a little cold, but still she swam on.

After a while she waded out of the water, feeling refreshed but oddly unsatisfied. She pulled on the dress over her wet skin, glad to remain cool for a few minutes longer in the warm breeze. She paused at the beginning of the path, smiling at her own foolishness.

She'd splashed, hummed, done everything but blow a foghorn.

But Justin Fuller preferred staring at a little green screen. Let that be a lesson, she told herself grimly as she walked past the cabin, a single glance confirming that Justin was just as she'd left him. A work-crazy, unwilling-to-be-involved male—shades of Martin Talmey!—was the last thing she needed to tangle with, this summer of all summers.

From now on, if Mr. Fuller wanted to learn how to relax, he could do it on his own.

CHAPTER SEVEN

"Gin."

Mrs. Koska's moon-shaped face lit up in a triumphant smile. Lydie frowned, putting her own cards down, and leaned forward to inspect the older woman's hand. "So that's where my king was," she muttered.

"I'm putting you in the poorhouse, honey," said Mrs. Koska. "That's another quarter . . ."

Lydie looked up as her companion's voice trailed off, a guilty expression on her face. Lydie knew immediately to shove the playing cards beneath the counter as a little girl with braided blond hair approached them, picture books in hand.

Cards and gambling went on at all hours in the Birchwood library, but it was considered bad form to be too blatant about it. Lydie checked out the child's books as Mrs. Koska affected to read the paper, and only when the braids disappeared through the library door did Lydie pay up her quarter.

It was her third consecutive loss in her first hour

at work, but a small price to pay for entertainment. The library, one large two-story room that had once been the town schoolhouse, was quiet as a tomb. So when the doors opened again, she looked up with hopeful expectation—only to blanch as she recognized the new arrival.

Justin Fuller had a pile of books in his hand. He was dressed in a pair of blue jeans that fit him well, she couldn't help but notice, and a white button-down, its rolled-up sleeves showing off the newly acquired sunburn on his muscular forearms. He hadn't seen her yet, absorbed as he was in scowling at the back jacket of the book on top of his pile.

Lydie prepared a suitably uninterested expression as he approached the desk. Justin put the books down on the counter with a thump, still frowning as he turned the top book around to face her.

"You know, it's bad enough that this is the only encyclopedic work on physics you have," he began. "But somebody's taken a pair of scissors to the very section I was—"

He stopped cold as his eyes met hers for the first time. Lydie decided the completely befuddled expression on his face was worth any amount of quarters lost to Mrs. Koska. "You?" he said, mouth still slightly agape.

"Yes," she said primly. "What seems to be the problem?"

"This is getting spooky," he said, shaking his head. "Lydie, is there anything you *don't* do in this town?"

"Sure," she said. "I don't fraternize with men who invite me to dinner and then neglect to show up."

Justin's eyes widened. Then he winced, averting

his eyes as he smoothed back his hair, clearly at a
loss for words.

Mrs. Koska had stopped shuffling her cards and
was looking on with great interest. "After you went
climbing all over the stacks to find these yesterday
afternoon," she said, shaking her head. "Pages torn
out, you say?" She clucked her tongue, looking from
Justin to Lydie.

"Damn," Justin muttered, meeting Lydie's eyes
again. "I meant to call. I'm really sorry, Lydie—but
something came up. It was kind of an emergency. The
factory that makes some hardware for me—"

"You don't have to explain," she said coolly. "It
really doesn't matter."

"Oh, yes, it does," he said, crestfallen, his eyes
glimmering with earnest remorse. "How could I have
been so stupid? I was on the phone for hours straightening out this mess, and by the time the phone was
free it was too late to call. And the guys at the office
have been after me all morning. I haven't gotten a
chance—"

"Really, it's all right," she said, feeling a twinge
of guilt herself for having been so hard-nosed and
thinking only about her own side of it. She hadn't
really considered that Justin might be an unwilling
prisoner of his own responsibilities.

"Let me make it up to you," he said quickly. "I
won't be working tonight. Are you free?"

"Sorry," she said automatically. "I'm having dinner
with my folks."

"Oh." He looked so severely crushed that, despite
her best intentions, Lydie felt her heart go out to him.
"How about lunch, then? When do you take a break?"

Lydie shook her head. "I just got here, Justin. And

I work the afternoon shift, straight through."

"It's a good system," he murmured, nodding. "I mean, I see what you're doing."

"You do?"

"Well, you'd get bored holding down one job full-time, so you work at a bunch of them, on alternate days." He smiled. "That's what I try to do with my own projects—juggle them around. It keeps my interest alive."

That was the perfect way to put it. Lydie found herself smiling back at him, though she hadn't meant to. Only when she felt Mrs. Koska reach past her to check in his books did she remember to affect detachment.

"Well, I'm sorry you couldn't find what you wanted," she said, efficiently halving the pile and beginning to remove cards as Mrs. Koska was doing. "But you know, out here in the wilds..."

"Don't be like that, Lydie," he said abruptly, in a quietly forceful tone that made her pulse pick up. "Why don't you invite me over to meet your folks?"

Lydie fumbled the book she was handing to Mrs. Koska, who was giving her an encouraging, motherly smile. Lydie cleared her throat. "You want to?" she asked dubiously.

"I want to get to know you," he said, his hand arresting hers as she reached for another card. Goose bumps without and trembling within was her unbidden response. This was wrong, all wrong. She'd just gotten her head straight about shutting Justin Fuller out of her life. And now...

"They're an odd bunch," she muttered, sliding her now-tingling hand out from under his. "Maybe I could make time for you later in the week."

"I won't embarrass you with any metropolitan snobbery," he said, smiling. "If that's what worries you."

What worried her more was the way she felt her body respond to his searching gaze. But it occurred to Lydie that if the man was secretly entertaining ideas of beginning a relationship—though he'd professed to want no part of such things—an evening with the Henleys might be just the thing to discourage him.

"You could probably use a decent home-cooked meal," she said grudgingly.

"Mrs. Henley's the best cook in Birchwood," Mrs. Koska interjected, beaming. Lydie and Justin turned to look at her. The librarian quickly addressed herself to collecting the book cards.

"You've got a good heart," Justin murmured to Lydie, his eyes twinkling mischievously. "Many a woman wouldn't be so forgiving."

Many a woman would be more careful about keeping her good heart intact, thought Lydie. "Come around eight," she said. "But if you're late—"

"In honor of the occasion," he said, "I'm going to unplug my computer from its battery pack."

The Henleys were the soul of hospitality, of course. Justin was accepted at the dinner table with an ease that worried Lydie. Mrs. Henley was convinced that all of Lydie's problems would disappear if Lydie would only find the proper man to set her straight, and Lydie didn't like the way her mother was eyeing the handsome stranger from New York.

What was he doing there, anyway? What was it he was after? Justin was polite, quiet, seeming to take everything in stride. Though she tried to see him as an interloper, a fudgie, a nuisance, he wasn't acting any way but . . . nice. It was frustrating.

Equally discomforting was the way he kept pumping her mother for details about Lydie's childhood. He seemed determined to find out all the lurid details of her precocious early years. Especially interesting, apparently, were the beginnings of her emergence as a female Picasso. This particular subject was as welcome to Lydie's adult ears as the sound of chalk on a blackboard.

"She was always a creative girl," Mrs. Henley was saying, passing the bowl of peas and carrots to Justin. "First there were the fingerpaints—"

"Mom," Lydie said hurriedly. "There's no need to go into—"

"Remember when she got her hands on those charcoals in the cellar, and turned practically everything in the house black?" This from Grandpa, who was chuckling with pride.

"Including my fresh linens," Aunt Helen added. "Henry, come down from there!" She rose abruptly from the table, cajoling her cockatoo to leave the corner rafters of the dining room.

"But the charcoal drawings were excellent," Mr. Henley reminded her. "Seven years old! Won first prize in that whatever-it-was contest in school. Hung 'em up in the glass display case."

Lydie was squirming in her seat. Justin, seated across from her, seemed delighted. He gave her a fond smile, then turned to watch Aunt Helen.

Having successfully coaxed the bird down and convinced it to alight on her extended arm, Lydie's aging relative walked slowly across the room. With the parrot still perched on her other shoulder, Aunt Helen

was eerily reminiscent of a circus juggler. Justin turned
back to Mr. Henley, his face betraying not a trace of
incredulity.

"Do you think Lydie got her talent from you folks?"

Mrs. Henley laughed, and Mr. Henley shook his
head. "Doubt it," he said. "I worked in radio all my
life. Couldn't draw a picture of an apple if you paid
me."

"But he's working on a book now," Mrs. Henley
said proudly. "He's writing biographical sketches on
everyone who lives in Birchwood year round."

"Three hundred and three of them," Mr. Henley
said.

"He's going to compile them and publish when the
job's done," Mrs. Henley added.

"Only got forty so far," said Grandpa.

"You never know who might turn up in the house
on a given day," Lydie told Justin, happy the topic of
conversation had shifted. "Or where Dad might turn
up, for that matter, with his tape recorder in hand.
Just two weeks ago, the *Enterprise* wrote up his unexpected appearance in the town fire truck when Car-
son's farmhouse went up in smoke."

"I was interviewing the chief when the alarm rang."
Mr. Henley shrugged. "More wine?"

Justin nodded. "Thanks." Aunt Helen had reen-
tered, sans parrot or cockatoo. She took her seat by
Justin and leaned forward to catch his ear.

"Henry's been in the rafters since this morning,"
she explained. "Lydie's grandfather was blowing up
things in the attic again."

Justin nodded, looking over to Lydie. But she wasn't
up to another explanation. He might think she came
from a house full of lunatics, but she supposed that

was just as well. She wanted him to keep his distance—didn't she?

"And what is it that *you* do, Mr. Fuller?" Grandpa asked. "I hear you're stuck inside that cabin with your face in a computer all day."

Lydie swallowed her sip of wine in a sudden gulp. You could count on Grandpa to be the soul of tact. But Justin merely smiled.

"I run a little company that makes software," he said. "Among other things."

"Software?" Grandpa's brow was furrowed. "What's that? Some kind of eating utensils?"

"It's the stuff you put in computers, Dad," Mr. Henley said.

"Justin's an inventor, too," Lydie added.

But the elder Henley looked singularly unimpressed. "Computers," he muttered. "Doesn't seem to me they're doing much to improve things, except maybe making life more complicated."

Silence reigned at the table for a moment. Justin seemed to be considering a comeback. But apparently he thought better of it, and merely looked uncomfortable.

Nasty as it might have been, Lydie couldn't help feeling a tiny bit of relief. Things weren't going so smoothly after all! Justin had been starting to look much too much at home. At last, some tension. Grandpa was infamous for his antitechnological bias.

Lydie gave Justin a wan smile to express sympathy for his predicament. Then her own loud yawn broke the silence. "Sorry," she said. "I haven't been getting as much sleep since I moved out of the cabin."

"Speaking of sleep, you ought to get your alarm fixed, Lydie," her father said. "Aunt Helen hasn't been able to rouse you for two days straight."

"I knocked on the door, just as you asked," Aunt Helen said.

"I know," Lydie said. "But I roll over and go back to sleep anyway."

"Ought to have Justin here fix you a foolproof alarm," Grandpa said. "Well, he's an inventor, isn't he?" he added, looking affronted at Lydie's sharp glance.

"Grandpa, really—"

"He's right, you know," Justin interjected. "I'm sure I could come up with something."

His eyes met Grandpa's, and Lydie felt her stomach sink. She could sense that a challenge was being made, one that Justin Fuller felt compelled to meet.

And so it was that the entire Henley family trooped up to Lydie's room directly after dinner. Justin, with a reel of fishing line, a few coat hooks, and a tape measure, began to busy himself there. Lydie looked on, helpless.

He attached the hooks at various points along the two walls between the door and the bed, then attached the fishing line to the doorknob. He ran the line along the walls, securing it on the hooks, then attached the other end to the bottom of Lydie's clock radio. He then formed an extra loop that he attached to the window shade by the bed, and yet another that he fastened to the edge of Lydie's covers. Finally he concocted some Byzantine contraption of lead fishing weights and hung them on the side of the bureau.

"The problem with the radio," Lydie offered, "is that if I set the volume too low, I sleep through it. But waking up to full-blast music ruins my whole morning."

Justin nodded. "This may take a few minutes," he informed his fascinated audience as he began to take apart the radio. He fiddled with its innards, replacing one part with a small metal disk lifted from her father's coffee tin full of electrical odds and ends.

"You're always up at seven-thirty sharp?" he asked Aunt Helen. She nodded as he continued his work. "And you try to rouse Lydie at ten to eight, when you're on your way back from feeding the pets?"

"That's right."

"Okay," Justin said, putting down his tools with a look of satisfaction. "Let's give this a try."

Despite her good-natured protests, Justin convinced Lydie to lie down on the bed, miming sleep with the covers over her. He had Aunt Helen posted in the hall with the door slightly ajar, and the other Henleys standing near the bed like a party of first-nighters at some avant-garde performance.

"Say it's eleven minutes to eight," Justin said, checking his watch. "Your alarm goes off."

Lydie listened, and, hearing nothing, opened one eye. "But it's—," she began, then stopped. There was the music, very faint. As she listened, it grew steadily in volume.

"Good work," Mr. Henley muttered approvingly. "He's rigged up a dimmer switch in there."

Justin nodded. "Fifteen seconds before seven-fifty, the radio reaches peak volume. Lydie, what do you do?"

Lydie, beginning to warm up to this charade, obligingly leaned over and pushed down the clock's button, abruptly ending the music.

"Aunt Helen?" Justin called.

A moment later, Aunt Helen stuck her head into

the room. "Lydie, dear," she said. "Time to get up."

"Thank you," Justin said, smiling. "Now pull the door shut."

Aunt Helen, cheeks flushed with pleasure at being a part of the evening's entertainment, did as she was told.

Lydie's clock radio, attached to the doorknob by the fishing line, began to slide silently down the long top of the bureau. As it gathered momentum, the shade started to rise, and Lydie felt the covers tugging, sliding off of her, pulled by the fishing line.

She sat up, startled. The radio alarm clock finally hit the wall with a quiet thud. The covers had been drawn past her knees, and the shade was two-thirds raised. As she stared at the weights Justin had attached to the side of the bureau, which had somehow regulated the movement of the line, she realized the alarm had been reactivated. Soft music emanated from it, rising in volume once again.

"So now what do you do?" Justin prompted.

A little dazed, Lydie climbed out of bed. She went to the radio and turned it off.

"You're now standing up in front of a shadeless window with the covers nearly off the bed," Justin said. "Think you're ready to stay awake?"

Lydie couldn't help smiling with delight as her parents and grandfather burst into spontaneous applause. Justin took a little bow, an insouciant grin on his face, as his eyes held Lydie's.

"Now, there's a man who's truly handy," Grandpa crowed. "Let go of this one, young lady, and you've lost your marbles."

"Grandpa," she sighed.

But he was already shaking Justin's hand and reviewing the mechanism with him as Aunt Helen hurried in to see. Things hadn't quite worked out the way Lydie had figured. She'd thought her family of misfits would throw Justin Fuller for a loop—but somehow he'd fit himself right in.

CHAPTER EIGHT

". . . AND HE MAKES his own ammunition. For skeet shoots, and quail hunting. Fireworks are just a sideline for Grandpa."

Justin nodded. They were standing on the edge of the drive to the Henleys' home, Justin having bid everyone good night. Grandpa had been the last to go in, after promising Justin he'd stop by the cabin the next day to help put in the outlets he needed.

"They're a great bunch of people," Justin said. "I'm glad you invited me over."

"You invited yourself," she said wryly. "But I'm glad you came. At least I won't have trouble getting up tomorrow morning."

Justin smiled. There was a warmth in his eyes that brought a smile to her own lips, along with a light-headed feeling. She reminded herself that she was supposed to be keeping her distance. But it was getting too hard to do that. The more sides she saw of Justin Fuller, the better she liked him.

"And what person will you be getting up to be

tomorrow?" he asked. "The cabdriver? The bartender? Or the librarian?"

"None of the above," she said playfully. "Tomorrow morning I suppose I'll be the Henleys' cabin caretaker."

"Really?" He looked pleased. "Coming to take care of me?"

"Not you," she said, giving him a wary look. "My garden. I don't suppose you've done any watering or pruning since your arrival."

Justin shook his head. "Sorry."

"And someone's got to check the pumps out back. One of them was leaking earlier in the summer. You probably wouldn't notice if the water main broke— unless the flood short-circuited your computer."

"You're right," he said, looking contrite.

Once again she had an impulse to brush the stray curl of hair out of his dark eyes. She shoved her hands in the pockets of her jeans. "You really do need a keeper," she murmured.

Justin shrugged. The slightly abashed look she was growing to recognize was now upon his face. They were silent for a moment as a warm breeze stirred the birch branches overhead. Justin's eyes seemed to catch a shaft of moonlight; they glimmered as he looked at her.

"Want to walk off some of your mother's cooking?"

"Okay." She fell in step beside him. Crickets sang in the tall grass by the side of the road. She felt a simmer beneath her skin as he took her arm for a moment to guide her over a small ditch in their path. His touch had a resonance that stayed with her after he'd let go, and it made her body tingle with energy.

Lydie wondered if all the women he encountered

reacted the same way to this soft-spoken but sharp-witted man whose touch was so electric, who was heart-stoppingly handsome but seemingly unaware of it. Was he a man of many affairs, with none that lasted? Or was he carrying on a myriad of relationships at once, even now, with none taking priority? The thought disturbed her.

"What was she like?" she asked suddenly. "The one that didn't work out?"

Justin cleared his throat, his eyes on the road ahead of them. "Joanne," he said quietly. "She was a bright woman, very talented. She was a systems analyst I met at MIT. Strong-headed and independent . . . to a point." He shook his head. "I think her big mistake was ending up dependent—on me," he added ruefully.

"You make yourself sound like the scourge of womankind," Lydie said. "What did you do that was so horrible? If you don't mind my asking," she added quickly.

Justin shrugged. "Well, I like to think my youth had something to do with it," he said slowly. "I got involved with her before I understood what involvement really means. We were engaged," he added, glancing at Lydie as they walked on. "But I was also engaged to the Juno machine, and to a bunch of other patents and projects at the same time."

"I get the picture," Lydie murmured. She did. In fact, she could imagine exactly what it must have been like. If she'd been upset over one broken date, what Joanne had dealt with must have been devastating . . .

"I thought I could juggle my relationship with her like I juggled all my many projects. That was insensitive to begin with." He sighed. "But in addition, I was a lousy juggler. It was bad enough, the times I left her up in the air—but then I wasn't there to catch her when she was coming down."

She could hear the pain in his voice. Lydie touched Justin's arm, sorry that she'd opened up what was clearly still a smarting wound. "I didn't mean to pry," she said softly. "You don't have to tell me any more."

"It's all right." His voice was still stiff with tension. "It was quite a few years ago. She's happy now—married a human-factors analyst from San Diego. And I learned my lesson."

He slowed, turning to look at her in the warm darkness. "At least I like to think I did," he said, his gaze holding hers. "But I'm not sure how much better at it I'd be now—a commitment, I mean. I've grown, but in many ways I'm still the same."

"But you sound like you know yourself pretty well by now," she said. "That's an important step, don't you think?"

Justin's lips curved in a faint smile. "Yes, I think," he said. "And I do know one thing. The next time I decide to give myself to a woman—really give—I'm going to give my all. I've learned the hard way what sharing your life with someone has to be about."

She felt the seriousness in his words, saw the depth of his conviction glimmering in his eyes. Her heart gave a tug, as if pulled into those dark depths. He was saying what she'd want any man to say, any man she loved . . .

But she didn't love Justin. Of course not. And if she understood him correctly, he didn't sound ready to make that commitment now. Why did she even care?

Because she was starting to care about him, she

realized, averting her eyes from his earnest gaze. "Well, you've learned a lot more than some," she said gently. She started to walk again, aware that they were nearly at the cabin by now, but reconciled to making the trip.

"It was similar for you, wasn't it—with that . . . Martin?"

Lydie nodded. "Martin and I weren't formally engaged," she said. "But there was talk of marriage. Just talk, unfortunately." She shook her head. "I'd like to attribute my mistakes to my youth, too."

Justin chuckled ruefully. "So here we are, a couple of old-timers—sadder but wiser."

Lydie smiled. "It does sound silly, I guess. To tell you the truth, I feel just as young. I'm practically starting my life over."

"So that's another reason for your wearing so many hats," he posited. "You're trying out livelihoods—to see what you'd like to do next?"

"In a way," she said thoughtfully. "I suppose I'm just treading water until I figure out my next move."

The thought of water reminded her of her nightly swim. They were standing at the entrance to the drive now, and by reflex, she looked in the direction of the lake. Justin followed her gaze.

"I don't suppose you'd like to come over," he said. "For some late-night gardening?"

Lydie smiled. "No wonder all your plants die on you," she said. "No, I'll wait for sunshine."

Justin checked his watch. "I must still be on West Coast time," he said. "I'm wide awake. What do you hicks do for kicks at this hour, anyway?"

She saw the teasing glint in his eye and raised a playfully threatening fist. "We beat up fudgies," she told him, "if they insist on acting superior. What would *you* be doing, wise guy, if you were back in the big city?"

"Honestly?" He furrowed his brow. "Well, in this heat, I suppose I'd be in a bathtub," he said. "Curled up with a good book."

Lydie laughed. "You always do your summer reading in the tub?"

He nodded. "Winter, spring, and fall too. I don't own a book that doesn't have some pages curled up from an unexpected dunking."

"I guess that's how you earned your honorary eccentric's license," she joked. "Any other unusual predilections you'd like to share with me?"

"I can think of a few," he said. "Some entirely natural ones..." Lydie felt her pulse beat faster as his eyes held hers and the innuendo sank in.

She cleared her throat. "I'll tell you what I'd be doing," she said. "Going for a swim—without a book."

Justin nodded. "And without a suit."

Lydie stared at him. As Justin smiled, looking a trifle guilty, she felt a blush begin to spread from the roots of her hair to the tips of her toes. "Oh, no," she murmured. "You didn't—"

"I had a strange hallucination last night—very briefly," he hurriedly assured her. "I happened to glance out my window when I was getting some spreadsheets from my suitcase, and I thought I saw a mermaid getting a moon-tan down by the dock. I didn't have time to investigate," he added quickly. "I had Denver on the phone and scads of columns to add up."

"Oh," she said, still scarlet.

"My calculations went awry," he said, "which confused Denver no end. But by the time I got them straightened out, that lady-of-the-lake vision was long gone."

"I shouldn't have gone in." She sighed. "But you see, it's a habit of mine."

"Pretty dark out there," he said. "And you can't really see much of the dock through the trees, you know."

As Lydie remembered it, the moon had been quite bright. But she appreciated his chivalrous lily gilding. "Right," she murmured.

"Seems a shame to break a habit," he said. "And it looked like fun to me. Maybe you wouldn't mind some company."

"Tonight?" The word came out in a little yelp.

"With suits, of course," he assured her, eyes twinkling. "I feel like I've been playing hooky since this afternoon as it is. This might be my last chance to do something absolutely unproductive," he informed her gravely. "They may need me in Denver tomorrow."

"Really?"

"You never know." He cocked his head, looking at her with comic hopefulness. "What do you say we go jump in a lake?"

Feeling a bit like a lascivious teenager, Lydie paddled through the water in bra and panties, having waited for Justin to go into the cabin to change before she disrobed at the dock. Though her mind had been full of shouldn'ts, the why-nots had overridden rationality.

The water felt marvelous, and the moon had swollen to ripe fullness in the sky. She missed the freedom of movement and the extra sensuality of swimming in the altogether, but modesty prevailed.

When she surfaced from a dive, Justin was at the dock. The shiver that went through her limbs at the sight of him in a swimsuit wasn't due to any chill in the water. What was the man doing with a physique like that? Wasn't a stratospheric IQ enough of a natural gift?

He dove in, splashing her as his body cut the surface. "Do you work out, or something?" she asked when he came up sputtering a few yards away.

"Tennis," he said. "Do you play?"

Lydie shook her head. "A little jogging, a little golf—but they don't have many putting greens in Manhattan."

Justin nodded. "This feels fantastic," he said. "No wonder you've made a habit of it."

He dove under the glimmering surface again and resurfaced close by, blowing a stream of water at her. Lydie ducked, laughing, and swam away—only to feel her ankle grabbed by a phantom from below. She kicked, escaped, and swam further.

They chased each other for a few minutes like seals at play, Lydie giving herself over to the fun of having a midnight playmate. Though she'd enjoyed her solitary swims, she realized now that she'd been missing this kind of friendly companionship all summer.

Friendly. As she waded into shoulder-high water, taking a rest, Lydie knew she was kidding herself. The erotic tension was there, fueling each underwater pursuit, each playful dunk. Although Justin wasn't trying to be seductive, their water play had a decidedly sensual tone. As she watched him back-paddle his way closer to her, she felt her heartbeat pound, felt the goose bumps of anticipation rise as they'd been rising on her skin since he first dove in.

She wanted him. She wanted to feel those soft lips capture hers again, wanted to feel the strong arms enfolding her as they had just days before. How could she deny it?

And now that he was the one holding back, she was experiencing a frustration she hadn't felt since she'd first gone out with "mature" boys in high school: that low-key but burning longing to fulfill an unfulfillable desire, to taste forbidden fruit—to be wicked, wonderfully wicked, and abandon herself when caution and prudence were what was needed.

"That shoreline over there—" Justin was wading over to her, gesturing at the dark shape in the distance, on the other side of the lake. "Is that the one in your painting?"

Lydie nodded, surprised he'd remembered. "Yes, I did the first sketches for it right here on the dock." He was close enough for her to imagine she could feel his body heat as they stood in the water. She glanced down, saw that the moon illuminated the white cups of her brassiere just breaking the surface, and folded her arms, self-conscious suddenly.

"Can I see more of your work?"

Lydie shook her head. "I'm afraid there's nothing to see. That painting was just an experiment, a fluke. I haven't done any serious work in years."

"That's the only thing I don't understand," he murmured. "You're an artist—a painter. If you've decided to get out of commercial graphics work, why don't you paint?"

The usual defensiveness threatened to tighten her throat and sharpen her tongue. Lydie forced herself to answer the question honestly instead of fighting it off. "I don't think I can make a living painting," she said evenly. "It seems too self-indulgent. I should be finding a suitable career."

"Suitable career?" he scoffed. "You sound like my guidance counselor in junior high. I'd already skipped two grades and was developing my own computer programs, but she was afraid I wasn't planning my future properly."

"I'm sure you were an exceptional case."

"So are you," he said. "You're immensely talented. You should give yourself the freedom to do what you do best."

"Freedom to starve?" she countered, then shook her head as he stood silently. "No thanks."

"But you're starving your spirit," he said softly.

His words were like a small, hot blade poised at her heart. He was right, of course. Ever since she'd stopped painting, she hadn't felt whole, somehow. There was an emptiness inside of her that nothing seemed to fill. And now, staring into his eyes, she felt the sadness well up inside of her again, a sadness it had taken so much effort to suppress . . .

"I can see it in your eyes," he murmured. "You shouldn't have that look, that little cloudiness in the clear, soft blue . . ."

Tears were gathering at the corners of those eyes now as she gazed up at him. She struggled to rein in her emotions. "I had been thinking," she whispered, "of giving it a try again. Just in the meantime . . ."

"Do it," he said, a husky fierceness in his voice that seemed to resonate right through her. "Why deprive yourself of the pleasure you get from doing what you want? Haven't you had enough sadness and disappointment? Do yourself a good turn, Lydie—let yourself go."

The earnest look on his face was so endearing that she felt herself begin to smile, the tears abating. This was what she'd been waiting for someone to say, she realized, her spirits lifting suddenly. She hadn't been able to give herself permission—she'd needed to hear it from someone else.

"You can always make ends meet," he went on, the enthusiasm in his voice buoying her even more. "At least while you try to find some sort of work that *can* support you, you can make yourself happier by doing your own work."

Lydie nodded. "I know," she said. "I've just been afraid to start . . . exposing myself again."

"Do it for you," he said. "Not for the galleries that didn't accept you, or the critics, or the 'them' that are always judging." He smiled. "I've been defying 'them' all my life. Believe me, Lydie, ultimately, it pays off."

She knew he was right. It was what she believed, secretly, but after the hard times she'd had in Manhattan, it had been easier to turn cynical—easier than pushing harder. She smiled, looking into those warm eyes that glowed with affection as he smiled back.

"You seem to know what you're talking about, Mr. Fuller," she said. "So what's it like, letting yourself go, doing what you want? Are you as happy as you can be?"

"Not quite," he murmured. "As a matter of fact, at the moment I'm feeling hypocritical."

"Why?" She tilted her face up, a teasing lilt in her voice, as she sensed his hesitation.

"Because I'm not doing what I want," he said huskily.

"Which is . . . ?" She held his eyes, feeling a shiver of anticipation as she saw the desire there.

"This," he growled, and gathered her into his arms.

His mouth was firm, delicious, tasting of the clean lake water and awakening each of her senses. She slipped her hands up his moist chest, parting her lips with an eagerness she couldn't disguise. She couldn't swallow the low murmur of delight that escaped her trembling throat as she felt his urgency meet her own.

He caught her head in one hand, gliding his fingers through her wet hair; his other arm slid around her back as he pulled her more tightly to his hard, smooth body. He tasted her lips with his tongue, then drank deeply of the sweetness of her mouth. Lydie felt a warm tide of arousal sweep through her with a piercing swiftness.

Very softly, he breathed her name, then found her mouth again to savor its shape more thoroughly. Gentle openmouthed nibbles gave way to deeper kisses as she clung to him, her mind clouding, body trembling with new sensations. He kissed her throat, seeking her pulse with his warm, soft lips, and she closed her eyes, leaning back in the cool water, breathless with excitement as his lips roved lower over her wet, tingling skin.

"Lydie," he murmured. "I know I shouldn't . . . but I can't stop myself."

"Then don't stop," she whispered, too flushed with excitement to halt the words. She was losing control—had lost it already as his hand slipped down her hip to the curve of her thigh.

Her own hands were forming trembling circles over

the wet tangle of hair on his chest, feeling for the beating of his heart. Her heart pounded feverishly as his lips kissed a warm, wet path from her neck to the valley between her breasts. His fingers found the clasp of her bra, suddenly become an irritating obstacle to the delirious pleasure those lips were bestowing.

Gentle hands slid the straps from her shoulders. She heard herself whisper his name unsteadily. Her breasts were aching for his touch. With torturous slowness, his hand rose to caress her wet nudity, fingertips easing higher until they met the delicate weight of one trembling globe.

Then his hand cupped her breast, thumb gently grazing its painfully erect point, and his lips stole over the soft, tingling skin. The spiraling sensations were nearly too much to bear. His lips found the taut, aching tip, licking and nibbling her there until she gasped with pleasure.

Then his hand closed over her breast again, and his lips sought hers with renewed urgency. She molded her body to his, shivering with arousal as his hard planes met her softer curves. Her breasts pressed against him, her hips meeting his beneath the water, and their tongues meshed in a suddenly savage dance of passion.

She could feel his hardness cradled in her thighs, feel the racing of his heart against hers, and she was woozily surprised that the water around them wasn't boiling. She was certainly aflame as his hands roved restlessly over her nakedness, and she clung to him even more tightly, breathless in a deepening kiss that seemed never to end . . .

But it did end. With a little shudder that told her he didn't find it easy, Justin gently pushed her from him as his lips left hers. Lips parted, eyes glazed with arousal, she stared into the dark pool of his eyes. Why had he stopped?

"Lydie..." His voice was a whisper. "Your lips are turning blue."

So? They could be turning into raspberry jelly, for all she cared. But she had to admit she did feel colder since he had withdrawn...

"And we're both going to turn into prunes," he went on, his expression so sober she suddenly smiled, still giddy from the voluptuous assault of those sensuous lips.

"Should we ... go inside?" she whispered, a little embarrassed by her own undisguised arousal.

"Sweetheart..." With an affectionate smile, he pulled her a little closer, gently kissing her on the forehead. "I feel I'm rushing you," he said softly. "I'm sorry. I don't mean to push you into doing anything you don't want to do."

Don't want to? she almost screamed. Every nerve ending in her body wanted ... *him*, without delay. Whatever was the man thinking of? Couldn't he tell?

"It's not fair to you," he was saying softly. "I should be giving you time to make sure ... that this is what you want. Because you know I can't make you any promises. I can't even say I'll be here for you any longer than tonight."

Startled as she was, Lydie couldn't help being touched to the core by his concern. A lesser man wouldn't have thought past the next minute, let alone the next morning. She stared at him, feeling the flush that suffused her body slowly lessen, her heartbeat begin to slow, as rationality seeped back into her befuddled brain cells.

"Justin Fuller," she murmured. "Are you the last of the urban gentlemen?"

His smile was almost bashful. "Maybe I'm a little old-fashioned," he allowed, "but I just thought I'd give us both a moment to . . . well, to take stock of our intentions. And I've got good ones—the best." He looked at her proudly. Lydie felt her heart go thump, and then melt into a little puddle of emotion, an emotion like . . .

Wrong word. The point was, he was right. She wasn't the kind of woman who just gave herself indiscriminately to the first man who made her pulse race. She'd only gone this far with Justin because she was starting to genuinely feel things for him—and that put her in a pretty vulnerable position. Somehow, this dearly genteel sexpot of a man had sensed all of that about her, and he was giving her an out.

"Justin?"

"Yes?"

"You're a good man," she said, folding her arms over her nakedness with a sudden sense of modesty.

"More like a damned fool," he muttered, his eyes sweeping her body with visible regret.

"Are you really planning on running out of town within the next twenty-four hours?"

Justin shrugged. "I have no plans. But my various commitments do have a way of . . . running off with me."

Lydie nodded slowly. "Well," she said thoughtfully. "Then maybe we should go a little slower. Like one day at a time."

"Right," he murmured. "But if you don't stop standing there like a wanton water nymph, I'm going to go back on my good intentions. With lightning speed."

Lydie smiled. Then she dipped down into the water and retrieved the soggy white lace bra. She held it, dripping, in front of her and gestured toward the cabin.

"What would you say to a hot cup of coffee—one for the road?"

"I'd bid it a grudging hello," he said. "It won't be as hot and inviting as those blue lips of yours, Lydie Henley—but I guess it'll have to do for now."

CHAPTER NINE

"MORNING, GOLDIES," Lydie said, lifting her watering can over the marigold pots. Peplinski's nursery was hazy with sunshine at that hour of the morning, and beads of water gleamed on the carefully tended rows of flowers as she made her rounds.

Peplinski's was her Thursday-morning job, and one that Lydie liked perhaps the best. For about four hours, this riot of gorgeous color, the moist air sweet with scents, was hers alone. It was like living in the middle of a Monet or Degas painting, and her eyes never tired of the artful combinations of hues that nature had designed.

The tomato plants in the corner were doing well, she noted, as she carefully wound a trailing vine around a stake she'd just planted. The jingling of the nursery's doorbells interrupted her investigation of a morning-glory jungle that was threatening to grow out of control. Lydie, wiping her hands on the dirt-smudged overalls she wore, headed for the front counter.

"Oh, no," said a familiar voice. "Now, this is too much."

Justin Fuller stood on the other side of the counter, arms folded, head shaking in disbelief. Lydie couldn't help grinning at the expression on his face as she faced him, elbows propped on the wooden counter top.

"Is it my fault you persist in following me around?" she teased.

"I had no intention of running into you," he said ruefully. "In fact, you're most definitely not supposed to be here."

"But I am," she insisted, "or Mr. Peplinski would be very upset."

"I'm the one who's upset," he growled. "I was planning to get you a surprise."

"Really? How nice." She smiled. "Surprise me now."

"What do you do, move from one store to the next? Are they all connected by a secret passageway? If I went next door, would you pop up behind the counter?"

"I wouldn't suggest you go into Judy's unless you're in the mood for a permanent or dye job," she said, smiling at his barrage of questions. "But, no, this is my only job on Juniper Street."

"Let's see—you've accounted for Monday through Thursday; does the cycle repeat, or do you have another job or two coming up?" He leaned his own elbows on the counter now, bending down to face her. "I just want to be prepared."

"One more," she admitted. "I'm tutoring a couple of local kids in drawing and painting." Her voice had somehow shifted into a lower, dreamier tone as she gazed into the soft dark velvet of his eyes, now so close to hers.

"Maybe I should sign up," he murmured, his voice gone husky, too.

"You're not a local kid," she replied softly, aware that his eyes were following the movement of her lips with great attention. She could feel the kiss coming before he leaned in closer, and her lips parted of their own accord.

Soft, moist skin brushed hers with the gentlest of touches, then moved away as a delicious tingle spread from her mouth to lower regions. "Good morning, Lydie," he breathed.

"Good morning," she echoed, disappointed as he straightened up with a look of slight chagrin.

"Couldn't resist," he murmured, then extracted a little seed packet from his back pocket. "Now, the reason I'm here," he said, suddenly gruffly formal, "is to purchase a flower pot and some dirt."

"You? Mr. Greenjeans himself?"

"All right, all right," he said, with a pained expression. "The thing is, I took a look at your garden this morning. Thought I might impress you with a little precaretaker watering. But I'm afraid I didn't look where I was stepping at first . . ."

"Oh, dear—what died?"

"Totaled a marigold," he admitted. "I tried to prop it up, but the thing wouldn't stay propped. So I found one of your seed packets lying around . . ."

The vision of Justin Fuller trying to coax a mangled marigold into remaining upright brought a giggle to her lips, but she managed to keep a straight face. "They're hardy plants, Justin," she assured him. "It might spring back in a few days."

"Well, I'd like to start a new one for you, just in case," he said. "All it takes is one of these seeds and some dirt, right?"

That the man who had invented a portable reading

machine for the blind was asking such a question was
hard to believe, but she nodded soberly. "I'll get you
a pot," she told him.

"You're still coming by, aren't you?"

"Sure. I get off around twelve-thirty."

"Good. Your grandfather should be done by then."

"Grandpa?" She turned back, startled.

"Yes, he's helping me install those three-prong outlets. That's my next errand, the hardware store. Say,
Lydie, you don't happen to work . . . ?"

"No," she said, smiling.

"Thought you might save me a trip," he said, eyes
twinkling. "You know, I never realized a pair of overalls could look so sexy."

"Flattery isn't going to get you a deal on dirt,
Justin," she said, doing her best to keep down a blush.
"I'll be right back."

"Lydie—" She turned back again. "Actually, I'm
glad I ran into you. Are you free this afternoon?"

She didn't think to be coy. "Yes, as a matter of
fact," she admitted. "After I finish a few chores at
your place."

"Do you have any interest in seeing some of the
work I do?"

"Sure. But how—"

"Tell you what, then. Bring a change of clothes
when you come, because we might have to leave fairly
quickly. Okay?"

"Okay," she said, nonplussed. "Where are we—"

"You'll see," he said breezily. "Hey, did the alarm
work?"

"Like a charm," she told him, and then hurried off
to get the pot he needed. What she wasn't about to
mention was how hard it had been to get to sleep.

After their moonlight swim, no amount of sheep counting had helped. And here she was, probably getting into deeper waters...

And she had the feeling it was too late to wade out.

Lydie was trimming back the long grass from the slate path around the back of the cabin when she heard it—a buzzing sound from the lake that was louder and lower than that made by any motorboat she knew of.

She stood up, shading her eyes with shears in hand, trying to locate its source. Grandpa had the back window open and was leaning out. He was the one who saw it first. "Good Lord!" he crowed. "Damn thing's gonna land right on this lake!"

Sure enough, there was an airplane, seemingly headed right for them. It was a seaplane, she realized as it descended, a twin-engine powder-blue Cessna. But what in the world was it doing landing on Lake Leelanau? Unless...

"Lydie?" Justin was hurrying around the side of the cabin, a briefcase in his hand. "I think you'd better get out of those overalls now."

"Don't tell me," she said, the realization sinking in. "That's our ride?"

Justin nodded. "Saves time. He's taking us to Chicago. Ever been?"

"Well, yeah," she said, watching with some trepidation as the plane roared over the lake's placid surface and touched down, looking as if it might barrel into the cabin as high plumes of water cascaded off its bottom runners. "Justin, do you ever do anything the way a normal person does?"

He gave her a worried look. "You're not afraid of flying, are you?" Lydie shook her head. "Good. Then you'd better change."

Lydie hurried into the cabin. She shooed Grandpa out of the way and stepped over his toolbox to reach the bathroom. Quickly she stepped into the dress she'd brought, then ran a brush through her hair and touched up her makeup.

When she emerged from the cabin, Grandpa and Justin were down at the dock, waiting with the rowboat. Only when she'd climbed in and they were approaching the seaplane did she think to ask what, precisely, she was getting herself into.

"We'll only be gone for the afternoon," Justin assured her. "I have to visit a laboratory and check on some things. You'll be back in time for dinner."

There was no time to press for details. Before she knew it, she was being helped aboard the plane by a crew-cutted pilot who looked as young as her younger brother, while Grandpa waved an amused good-bye from the rowboat.

"Isn't he a little young to be doing this?" she whispered to Justin as he adjusted her seat belt for her in the narrow, four-seat interior.

"Air force," Justin told her. "Relax."

Relax?

Nervousness aside, she couldn't help but be caught up in the excitement as they lifted off again. She'd never seen the lake from the air. It was fascinating to see the familiar contours of the shore from this great height, and she delighted in pointing out landmarks through the little porthole window as Justin looked on.

The bright blue of the lake was receding, followed

by a strip of greenery, then the deeper navy of Lake Michigan. Soon Lydie was used to the gentle, steady vibration of the small craft. It seemed perfectly natural to eat one of the wrapped sandwiches Justin handed her, and to sip iced tea, as the lake spread out below, the distant shadow of the Cessna visible as it crossed little specks of white sailboats.

And there was a different kind of excitement she felt as she sat next to Justin in the plane. It came from the look in his eyes when they swept over her, the electric jolt she felt when his hand touched hers, however briefly. There was a secret they seemed to be sharing, unspoken, that hovered beneath the surface of their casual conversation, and it made her heart beat faster in the silences between the words.

Justin had dressed for the trip in his usual jeans and button-down. His hair was unkempt as ever. But Lydie couldn't shake the feeling that someone who could afford to be chauffeured about in a seaplane, had been holding out on certain particulars about his life.

"It's kind of a pet project of mine," Justin was explaining in answer to her questions sometime later. They were beginning a descent toward the skyscraper-lined shore of Chicago. "And it's developed a little hitch. We've patented a microchip with one particular silicon chemical coating that's supposed to do the job, but the lab here that started making them in bulk isn't reproducing them properly."

"And what's the job the chip's supposed to do?" she asked.

"It's part of a chain of components that ultimately conducts the vibrations of human speech through a computer," he said. "We're trying to perfect a voice-activated machine."

"You mean a computer that responds when you talk to it?"

Justin nodded. "No keyboard. You talk, it writes—or calculates. Whatever function you want."

"That's . . . something," she said, at a loss for a better superlative. "I mean, it sounds like science fiction."

"It might still be," he said gloomily. "Our test models in Denver worked fine, but as soon as we started running off copies, we hit a wall. If I can't locate the specific problem area, we might have to rethink the whole structure."

The enormity of Justin Fuller's work was beginning to sink in. As her mind reeled, the plane took a dip, and she couldn't ask any more questions. They were skimming the lake's surface, headed for shore.

Lydie realized he'd been downplaying his various projects to a greater degree than she'd suspected. But she still wasn't ready for the red carpet that Chicago rolled out when they reached solid ground.

First there was the mile-long silver limousine waiting for them on the dock. No sooner were they in its plush, air-conditioned interior than the phone in the back seat rang, and Justin was soon involved in a technical conversation she couldn't begin to comprehend.

The next shock was the look of the plant that apparently worked for Justin's "little company." It was a high-tech, modernistic sprawl of glass and concrete that occupied a full city block in downtown Chicago. They were ushered inside by men in suits who treated

Justin, attired in jeans and a shirt sans tie, as if he were visiting royalty.

Lydie was glad she had worn a dress that was a shade more than informal. She walked at Justin's side down carpeted halls of white walls and muted conversation, as various technicians in smocks hurried in and out of doorways. She felt a vague sense of disbelief and a growing irritation.

Why hadn't he told her what to expect? Didn't he realize the effect all of this might have? Was she supposed to take it in stride—as he apparently did? Was she expected to be blasé about a project—one of many, apparently—that obviously involved God-knew-how-many millions of dollars?

There was a workspace the size of an airplane hangar in the main building, where teams of men worked over gleaming Formica tables, silver instruments in gloved hands. Lydie took the tour, a few steps behind Justin and his guides, still dazed at the vastness of the place, the amount of manpower and machinery that was being brought to bear on . . . Justin Fuller's "pet."

At a certain point, she was politely requested to wait for his return in a private suite outside a conference room. She caught a glimpse of a group of men who looked like members of the *Fortune* 500—rising to greet her tousled-haired companion—and then the door shut behind him.

A friendly secretary served her coffee and pastry. Lydie wandered around the office looking at photo reproductions of various machines, one of them the Juno 3000 Justin had mentioned that night in the White Finch. Apparently Fullstar Enterprises was responsible for enough software to stretch from coast to coast, and for a word processor named Joni. Lydie thought of Justin's Joanne and felt a completely irrational jolt of jealousy. And apparently Justin *owned* this place! That wasn't what he'd implied before.

When Justin emerged some twenty minutes later, his look of worried preoccupation had lifted somewhat. He took Lydie by the arm as they followed some executives down yet another labyrinth of halls. "Sorry to abandon you like that," he said quietly. "We're almost done here."

Lydie nodded stiffly. She was suddenly not in the mood for chitchat. "Why the sudden rush, Justin?" she asked. "Couldn't this humongous staff of yours attend to the problem while you were out of town?"

"Deadlines," he said. "If we don't work out the snag, we stand to lose millions. The machine's already been preordered all over the country. Some of our prospective customers have started to apply a lot of pressure."

"Like who, for example?"

Justin cleared his throat. "The Pentagon..."

That did it. Lydie merely nodded and clamped her lips shut. For all she knew, he could be working for the CIA. He might be a billionaire. He might own IBM.

When you came right down to it, she had absolutely no idea who he was. She didn't know Justin Fuller at all.

CHAPTER TEN

IT WAS DUSK on Lake Leelanau when the hum of the seaplane's motor faded away, and Lydie followed Justin up the path from the dock. At the path around her garden, he paused, turning to face her with a perplexed expression.

"You've been awfully quiet, Lydie," he said. "What is it?"

"What's what?" she countered, still unwilling to open up.

Justin sighed. "What are you angry about?" he asked, his eyes holding hers. "I'm sorry if I was a bit caught up in things down there. I had hoped you'd find it interesting, though . . ."

"It was fascinating," she said evenly. "Now maybe you'd like to fill me in on a few details."

"What would you like to know?" he asked, a picture of innocence.

"Everything!" she exploded. "Good grief, Justin! Why didn't you give me some kind of indication, any-thing—from the look of things you could be running

110

half of the Western world with that place at your disposal! I mean, I knew you were a busy man, but—"

She stopped, momentarily speechless. Justin had that sheepish look on his face that was guaranteed to melt all hearts, but she tried to resist melting—at least until she'd found out something more about this infuriatingly mysterious man.

"Well, it's kind of technical," he said, looking like a boy caught with his hand in the cookie jar. "I mean, if I tried to explain all of the patents I'm involved with—"

"I'll settle for the general picture," she said. "For starters—do you own that place?"

"In a manner of speaking, yes."

"And you're personally worth . . . megabucks, aren't you?"

Justin cleared his throat. "I do okay."

"Okay?"

"Fullstar Enterprises aims to build businesses of some hundreds of millions of dollars over the next few years," he said with a slightly pained expression. "Look, don't hold it against me, now, all right?"

"Hold it against you?" she echoed weakly. "Justin, the only thing I've got against you at the moment is your unwillingness to—to tell me about yourself! I mean, I've confided in you enough to feel like an open book. But the way you've been covering up, it's not just modesty. What is it? Why all the secrets?"

"Well, I didn't want to . . ." Justin sighed. "People sometimes get the wrong idea. I mean, you and your family are regular folks. You lead normal kinds of lives. And me, I've been . . . a misfit ever since I can remember. I guess I was seeing if I could, well . . ."

"Pass?" she suggested, unable to keep an incredulous smile from her face. "For a regular kind of guy? Oh, Justin..."

"Well, I know I didn't make such a good first impression," he said gruffly. "You thought I was a vain city slicker to begin with. So I did try to keep quiet about...things so you wouldn't think I was a total oddball."

"Justin, you couldn't pass for Joe Normal if you tried," she said ruefully. "But that's not bad. It's not a bad thing at all."

Justin looked at her with a faintly mischievous smile. "So it doesn't bother you to hang out with a screwball scientist who's turned himself into an industry?"

"I think I can handle it," she said wryly. "In fact, I'd much rather you told me all about your work—as much as I can understand—and about how you got to be where you are at—" She stopped. "Justin, I don't even know how old you are."

"Thirty-three," he said. "Okay, Lydie, I'll put on the coffee, and you can ask me anything you like."

Coffee making was apparently the one culinary skill Justin Fuller possessed, although he admitted to a passing acquaintance with French toast. Lydie started with random inquiries and then moved from vital statistics to a profile of childhood as they sipped the coffee on the little porch at the cabin's front.

His father was a professor at Columbia University, his mother a classical musician. When his prodigious talents became evident, they'd allowed him to be a quiz kid on a national radio program, where he systematically won the biggest prizes, astounding adults with his memory and imaginative skills.

He'd skipped third and eighth grades, and had entered college at sixteen. He'd already invented his first software program in high school, with a friend, yielding him a sizable income that more than paid for his own tuition. He was the youngest to graduate in his class at MIT.

He talked of a life that was achievement building upon achievement—from his first business venture with a major corporation at twenty-two, to his successful work on the reading machine, prompted in part by his father's partial blindness and the older Fuller's dissatisfaction with existing machines of that type.

"Doesn't sound like you had much time to play softball with the guys on your block," Lydie noted.

"Nope." Justin shrugged. "I was ahead but behind at the same time all my life, if you know what I mean. I was doing algebra when the rest of my class was still on multiplication tables, but I wasn't old enough to drive a car when the other guys in school were cruising into the city on weekends." He shook his head ruefully. "I was academically advanced, but too young to date the girls in my class."

They must've thought you were cute, though, Lydie thought. "You know, I had a similar kind of school life, in one sense," she reflected. "I was always sketching and drawing, when my friends all had graduated from doll playing to going out on dates. Of course, my folks accepted me whatever I did, but I always felt a little left out of the social circle."

Justin nodded. "My social circle was textbooks, machines . . . hackers and nerds."

"Sounds lonely," she said.

"Not really. I've always been so busy, I've never had time to look back, to think about what I may have missed," he said quietly.

"But your life has been exciting," she protested. "Look at all the different kinds of things you're involved in—and the numbers of people you must deal with all the time."

Justin shrugged. "I'm not complaining. But every now and then, I wish I could live a normal week, with normal times to goof off—go fishing," he added with a grin. "It's been a real challenge, taking this vacation. I keep thinking if I'm not at the helm every moment, all the projects I'm involved with are going to go down the tubes."

"You're only human," she said. "And you went fishing. Did the sky fall? No."

"No," he said, smiling. "And I really enjoyed it, thanks to you . . ." Justin's finger briefly traced the line of her cheek as she looked at him, the gentle touch making a shiver run through her. Again, she found herself mesmerized by the warm glow that emanated from his searching gaze. It seemed that she couldn't stop looking at him . . .

"Well, did you make any headway today?" she asked. "Can you afford to relax tonight?"

"We narrowed down the bottleneck area to the coating on the chip. There's nothing for me to do until we get some lab test results sometime tomorrow."

"Then you can go back to your vacation," she said. "Shut down your overworked brain cells for the night."

"All right, guardian angel." He smiled. "Got any other suggestions? What would you be doing on a night like this to unwind after a day's work?"

Lydie considered. "Watch an old movie on TV," she said. "But you do that, don't you? From time to time?"

Gravely, Justin shook his head. "The only TV

screens I look at are computer screens," he admitted.

"Really?" Lydie sighed. "Boy, you really do need a crash course in mindless unwinding. Well, you want to give it a try?" She gestured at the cabin. "There's an old back-and-white portable in there that's perfect for any film made before 1950."

"Sounds like fun," he said. "What's on?"

"As a matter of fact, one of my favorites," she said, remembering. *"Casablanca.* But I've seen it twenty times, and you've probably—" She looked at him. "No? You're kidding."

"Humphrey Bogart's in it," he said. "That's all I know."

"My Lord," she murmured. "A *Casablanca* virgin. All right, Justin Fuller—we're going to give you a classic, regular-folks, quiet evening at home. Complete with the requisite buttered popcorn."

Justin checked his watch. "Now who's thinking like a city person? Where do you expect to get popcorn at this hour?"

Lydie shook her head. "Hopeless, hopeless," she muttered. "Justin, we're going to *make* popcorn. That's part of the fun—think of it as a normal native ritual," she teased.

Back inside the cabin, Lydie got out the permanently grease-stained pot she always used for popcorn popping and set to work measuring kernels and melting butter while Justin set up the TV opposite the couch in the living room. She continued quizzing Justin about his life in the suburbs of Manhattan, and supplemented his anecdotes with stories of her own life.

He listened and laughed as they compared notes on their respective childhoods that didn't conform to the norm. He reduced her to fits of giggles as he gave her glimpses of the incompetence that could inadvertently reign in the highest circles of industry.

By the time they were settled down on the couch together, a giant bowl of hot buttered popcorn between them, Lydie felt more comfortable with Justin than she'd ever imagined she could. He was good company, but more than that, he was sweetly thoughtful, responding seriously, sensitively, to the things she said, and alternately prone to sudden bursts of absurdist humor that kept them both bubbling over with laughter.

She'd uncorked a bottle of red wine long lain dormant in a kitchen cabinet, and the warmth of the wine, the touch of his hand, the glow in his eyes combined to make a heady mixture as they settled back to watch the movie. It seemed only natural when his arm slipped around her, only right that her head should find a tender cradle in his shoulder.

The sultry summer air seemed to seep under her skin as they lost themselves in the familiar romantic terrain of Casablanca, where piano music tinkled in smoky Rick's Cafe, and passion simmered in the black-and-white shadows at the desert's edge.

CHAPTER ELEVEN

THE GREAT LOVE of Humphrey Bogart's life was airborne, flying off with another man. He stood on the tarmac below, trench coat collar up, ubiquitous cigarette dangling from his lips as he turned to Claude Rains with an ironic smile.

"Louie, I think this could be the beginning of a beautiful friendship..."

The two men walked off together into the fog on the Casablanca airstrip, and Lydie sighed as the music swelled. Simultaneously, Justin let out a sigh of contentment. She turned to him, smiling, then averted her eyes, aware that her cheeks were still wet with tears.

"That was wonderful," he murmured, then leaned forward, concerned. "Hey, are you all right?"

"Oh, I'm just a sap," she said, quickly wiping the corners of her eyes with the torn corner of a crumpled napkin. "No matter how many times I see this silly picture, I still get all choked up."

"Lydie, I don't blame you." His voice was husky

with affection as he held out another, less mangled napkin. With a look of sympathy, he watched her blow her nose, then grimaced as he tried to sit up straight.

"Oh, dear—your arm," she muttered, seeing that he was bending it carefully. "I'm sorry."

"Don't be. It fell asleep, is all." He rubbed it, still watching her as she dabbed at her eyes.

"You must think I'm an idiot," she said, sniffling, supremely self-conscious.

"Not at all," he said softly. "I'll tell you a secret. The last time I saw a movie in a theater was in seventh grade. It was *West Side Story,* and I was with a girl I had a terrific crush on. Her name was Judy Wernamacker." He smiled, handing her her glass of wine. "It was the first time I'd been out with a girl without a chaperon—it was a Sunday matinee—and I was doing everything I could to impress her with how mature and adult I was."

Lydie smiled, picturing Justin the tousled-haired computer mogul as a nervous little boy at the movies, then nodded in agreement as he leaned over to turn off the television set.

"Well, when Tony died at the end, and Maria was weeping, so was most of the audience—including me. But a boy isn't supposed to cry," he reminded her gravely. "I must have gone through every subtle contortion in the book to keep those tears from coming. Just before the lights came on, I rubbed my eyes to make sure not a trace of emotion was visible."

Justin chuckled, thinking back. "So, wouldn't you know it? Judy Wernamacker, who's been blubbering away with both faucets going, turns to me in a rage. 'What kind of a person are you?' she said. 'How could you watch that and not even cry?'"

Lydie laughed, then took a sip of wine. "I don't see any tears on your face now," she teased. "Didn't you learn your lesson?"

"Sure." He smiled. "But I'm a grown-up now—and men *my* age certainly never, under any circumstances, cry at the movies."

Lydie laughed again, leaning back against the couch. But as she looked at him taking a sip from his wineglass, she could suddenly imagine with greater clarity the hardship Justin must have endured as a child prodigy.

He *had* been asked to act like an adult, fast—expected to be as emotionally mature as he was mentally advanced. No wonder he tended to be guarded about his feelings. Now, the shyness she'd sensed in him, and hadn't been able to understand, seemed only natural.

"It's not easy, bottling yourself up," she mused aloud. "I've done my share of that, especially when I first went to New York. I had to learn how to be defensive in a hurry."

"You seem to have unlearned it pretty well," he said.

"Well, the way of life's a lot different here," she said. "There's not so much to be guarded about."

Justin nodded. "It's nice," he said simply. "I'll miss it."

"Do you know when you're leaving?" she asked, feeling a pang of anxiety. Suddenly she couldn't imagine *not* being here with Justin, and the thought made her feel strange inside.

"I'm not sure," he said. "But even when I do . . ." He leaned forward, a mischievous twinkle in his eye. "Shweetheart," he murmured in a pretty good Bogart imitation, "we'll always have Paris."

His quote from the movie gave her heart a little tug. Her smile faded as their gazes locked. His hand had settled briefly on her knee, and it stayed there now, spreading a shiver through her at the casual but intimate contact.

Justin slowly leaned in closer. His other hand reached out to gently stroke her cheek, fingers tenderly playing with a wisp of hair around her ear. Lydie felt the desire that had been simmering in her blood all evening rise within her as his eyes glimmered with arousal, silently posing an unspoken question.

Instinctively she wet her lips with her tongue, the warmth from his gentle grasp suffusing her, fanning the flame that seemed to flicker with renewed strength between them. The feeling swelling up in her couldn't be ignored any longer as he watched her, waiting. The incandescent glow of his eyes emboldened her, and her hand stole out to cover his.

As the delicate caress of his fingertips on the soft skin of her neck provoked another shiver, she found herself, as though hypnotized, moving her face to guide his hand lower. Slowly his palm shifted downward, his fingers tracing the line of her neck, pausing at the little pulse at its base.

His eyes held the question; his lips parted slightly with a breathless expectation that matched her own. Her eyes gave him the answer he was seeking. Her pulse beat strongly beneath his warm fingertips, and without a word, his lips dipped down to meet hers.

Lydie's lips parted instinctively to taste the sweetness of his mouth, a shivery current coursing through her from his tender touch. Justin's mouth left hers, hovering inches away. Without thinking, she moved forward, her lips still parted.

Then, seeing a smile lift the corners of his lips, she was embarrassed by how clearly her desire had shown itself.

"Lydie...," he murmured. "Do you want me... as I want you?"

She'd been fighting it too long. Involvement... noninvolvement. Meaningless words. All that mattered was now, and the feelings she felt. "Yes," she whispered. "So much..."

He bent his face to hers again, lips brushing each eyelid, kissing the lashes with a tenderness that made her tremble. His hand lightly traced the line of her neck. Lydie swallowed, the pounding in her blood making thought, let alone speech, difficult.

She wanted to let him know, somehow, that she was more than ready, no matter what happened, no matter what lay beyond this magical moment they were sharing. She'd never felt so achingly expectant, so vulnerable with sheer arousal.

"Justin," she whispered as she felt his hesitation. "It's all right..."

He lifted her chin with his thumb and forefinger, his eyes gazing into hers. "Is it?" he murmured. "Is it all right that I've fallen for you, head over heels? All right to love you...?"

She nodded, her heart beating with hummingbird speed. Love. It was a word she hadn't wanted to think about, to acknowledge, but she knew the feeling, had already felt it growing within her. Would he love her with the tenderness she felt? Or with the fierceness that she felt as well?

"I'm going to love you right," he murmured, as if he'd read her secret thoughts in her eyes. "It's too late to hold back now, too late to stop..."

His lips brushed hers in a featherlight kiss. "I've been wanting you since the moment I saw you." His voice was a husky, velvet whisper. "Let's make it last..."

He bent to graze her upturned chin with his lips. The light touch of skin to skin made her blood whirl in heated excitement. Her mouth moved eagerly to his. Her hands slid past his collar to grasp the curls of his soft, dark hair.

As Lydie pressed herself closer to meet him with an uninhibited urgency, his mouth commanded hers more forcefully, exploring her in a tantalizingly slow and sure possession. He murmured her name again, and she felt her desire mount in an uncontrollable surge.

As his body moved sensuously against hers, she clung to him, and a moan caught deep in her throat. Lydie slid her hands slowly from his neck to feel the warm hardness of his chest. Their kiss lengthened. Her hunger increased. She reveled in the feel of the burly chest hair beneath her fingertips as they played at the collar of his shirt.

Justin's strong hands gathered her closer to him. She shivered as his fingers traced the line of her spine through the soft material, restlessly gathering her shirt up until it came untucked. His hands slipped slowly along the naked skin beneath.

His lips broke from hers. "I've been needing to feel you in my arms again," he murmured. "You're sure you don't mind?"

Mind? Lydie couldn't help smiling at his concern. She was delighting in the way he prolonged each moment, anticipation making the air electric. Now he bent to kiss the soft nape of her neck, then planted a hot, moist trail of kisses from chin to collarbone.

The delicious ache of pleasure was nearly too much. She shifted her weight on the couch, her hips moving instinctively against his. Justin's hands stole to open the top button of her shirt with painstaking slowness. Then he kissed each inch of newly revealed skin, bringing it to vibrant life beneath his soft wet lips.

Tingle by tingle, he kissed a path to the hollow beneath her breasts, still half-hidden under the unbuttoned shirt. Lydie's mouth fell open in protest when his lips at last left her skin. The tips of her breasts were swollen, rubbing against the taut cloth. Though she was reveling in the slow building of their passion, the clothing suddenly seemed an irrational restriction. She wanted to feel all of him against her.

His arms gently released her then, and their eyes locked in a wordless communication. Justin's hand crept out to tug at the buckle of her belt.

"If you're going to stop me, stop me now," he murmured, his voice a rasp of arousal. She shook her head. Instead, she reached to grasp the clasp of his jeans, delighting in his quick intake of breath as her fingers fumbled at the belt.

They both seemed seized with the same impatience. Both smiled as they started a wordless race to disrobe. Her shift fell to the floor, then his. Zippers unzipped, and pants rolled down past naked thighs in haste.

For a long moment after this frenzied flurry, he gazed at her as she lay back on the couch, his eyes drinking in her nudity with obvious delight. "Lydie," he breathed in a ragged whipser. "You're so incredibly beautiful . . . How could I have deprived myself a moment longer?"

Her eyes, too, wandered over his body, taking in each muscular curve and plane with pleasure. Suddenly emboldened, she pulled him to her. He hovered above her, his gaze lingering on the quivering pulse at the base of her throat. He paused to drink in the full roundness of her breast, to savor the lines of her taut belly, the curve of her thighs.

The tips of his fingers slowly traced each curve, hands moving from shoulder to breast. Lydie exhaled softly as his hand gently closed over one trembling soft mound, his palm slowly circling its swollen tip, sending an exquisite shiver of arousal through her.

His thumb teased the nipple into hard awareness as his face dipped to plant arousing kisses on her throat, then moved lower. His warm breath sent tremors through her, and she moaned as his tongue found the sensitive peak. His tongue tasted her, lips possessing the taut tip, teeth and mouth nuzzling her until the moan lengthened and deepened.

Lydie tangled her hands in his thick dark hair. Her back arched as the feelings surging inside of her grew, threatening to burst. He kissed and nibbled one breast, then the other, his hand cupping and caressing each in turn.

Her breath came in ragged gasps now as she moved, eyes closed tightly, beneath him. Her fingers ran restlessly through his hair as his mouth kissed a fiery moist trail between her breasts. He lowered himself, arms sliding around her thighs, hands molding the curve of her buttocks, as his lips covered the soft skin of her stomach with kisses. Then his lips fanned the warm center of her arousal into an arching, white-hot flame.

Lydie heard herself murmuring his name again and again as he tantalized her with playful strokes of lips and tongue. Even when his lips left her trembling skin at last, her body quaked. She clung to him, gathering the warm strength of his body to her with an exultant sigh.

Now her hands feverishly felt every line of his body against hers. Passion was overtaking them, caution left far behind. She covered his chest with kisses until it was he who moaned with pleasure. She explored his body boldly, caressing him with tender, teasing touches until he cried out as she had.

She could feel the sweat gathered at the back of his neck, and the slickness of her own body. When the couch gave a loud squeak of protest beneath their weight, they both froze, then began to laugh together in the darkness.

"Isn't this couch a little ... adolescent?" he whispered in her ear. "I keep thinking your father's going to show up at the door with a shotgun."

"Justin," she reproached him. "He knows I'm a big girl now. But I know what you mean ..." She kissed a bead of sweat that was gathered at his chin. "It seems too hot for a bed, though," she whispered.

"Hot indeed," he sighed, a lascivious glint in his dark eyes. "You know what I'd like to do?"

"Tell me."

"Another confession," he murmured, his fingers tracing a line of sweat down her neck. "I've never made love ... in the great outdoors."

She widened her eyes in comic shock. "But Justin," she teased. "Isn't that a very *un*regular thing to do?"

"It sounds wonderfully natural to me," he said. "Come on."

With a deep-throated growl, he grabbed hold of her, swooping her up into his arms. Aloft, she laughed, her arm tight around his neck. She loved the feel of his naked strength against her as he carried her to the doorway.

The night breeze felt heavenly on her moist skin as they stepped to the lawn, the evening sky ablaze with twinkling stars. A chorus of crickets seemed to welcome them. Justin carried her easily to the grassy knoll on the cabin's side, then gently lowered her down.

Lydie pulled him down with her, suddenly impatient with desire. When his lips found hers, she returned the kiss with an untamed passion that matched his own. She reveled in the weight of his smooth, rugged body fitting to her softer curves, the wonderful roughness of his burly chest hair against her breasts.

He murmured a wordless sound of pleasure as he fitted his body to hers in the soft grass. They sank into a long deep kiss of breathless urgency. Curve moved to curve; skin melded to skin.

She'd never known this kind of pleasure before, a prolonged, sweetly savage desire that ebbed and flowed, ever-building between them. He led her, panting, to a plateau of arousal, only to hurtle her higher, urging her with eager lips and hands to even greater joys.

She saw the stars glimmering above, felt the earth seem to move beneath her. She was awed by her own passion as his gentleness gave way to a surer, stronger touch, a touch that spurred her on to more reckless abandon. Each kiss and caress brought them closer, until at last, with an exultant groan, he merged with her at last.

Lydie moved sinuously with him, savoring the feel of his hard strength within her yielding softness. The throb of her pulse mingled with his heartbeat pounding against hers. Together they sought the perfect rhythm, found the tempo of the dance. He pleasured her with knowing movements and she answered him in kind, sharing every intimacy to the fullest.

Soon there was no prolonging every moment. There was no stopping the gathering momentum. She wrapped herself tightly around him and left gravity behind. She heard him whisper her name, heard his name torn from her lips. The stars flared, disintegrated, and they hurtled, weightless, into ecstasy.

CHAPTER TWELVE

"LYDIE?"

"Umm?"

"I don't think it's possible to be happier than this, do you?"

"Nope." She sighed.

"There's only one problem..."

"Yes?"

"I don't want it to stop."

"Oh..." She closed her eyes, loving the feel of his hands gently tracing circles on her back as she lay on top of him. "It doesn't have to, does it?"

"Maybe not," he murmured. "We'll see..."

"Yes, we'll see," she whispered dreamily, luxuriating in the feel of his skin against hers, the warm darkness around them both like a silken cocoon.

"Lydie?"

"Ummm..."

"There is one more problem."

"What's that?"

"I can't see the shore anymore."

Sleepily, she raised her head from the warmth of Justin's chest, looking at the dark water that surrounded them. "S'okay," she murmured, snuggling close to him again.

It had been his idea to cool off in the lake afterward, but hers to take the rubber raft out. It was big enough for the two of them to lie in comfortably, their feet just trailing in the water. It felt marvelously safe and secure, their own little island floating off the coast of the world.

Time seemed suspended as they huddled together, his arms encircling her in the warm darkness. How long had they lain together in the soft grass? How many words of love had they whispered, skin to skin? She didn't know, or care, feeling blissfully fulfilled as they floated on, the water lapping quietly over her toes.

Sleep stole over her and then receded, dreams merging with reality. He was telling her stories of stars and quantum physics, inventing marvelous futures for them and everyone, then caressing her into lazy, pulsing arousal for more exultant love play.

They overturned the raft, of course, and swam through the cool water, through the darkness of an endless night. And then they were on the raft again, wrapped around each other under a canopy of stars.

She dreamed again, and imagined siren voices calling them from a distant shore. The colors of the sky had shifted suddenly to a lightened hue, and someone was urging her awake—

"Lydie Henley! Is that you?"

Not a dream. Startled, she lifted her head, staring up woozily in the direction of the voice, feeling Justin stiffen underneath her. A familiar face, upside down, was gazing at her.

"Really, now, Miss Henley . . ."

Good Lord. It wasn't a dream, it was a waking nightmare. She was looking at the face of Andy Kolker, friend of the family and one of Birchwood's men in blue. And then Justin was shifting suddenly, shielding her, and she couldn't see much at all.

"Morning, Officer."

"Morning," drawled Kolker. "Don't believe we've met."

"I'm Justin Fuller. I've been renting the Henleys' cabin?"

"Oh, that's right."

Heart pounding, Lydie winced at the insufferable absurdity of men and manners. Peeking beyond Justin's shoulder, she could see that they had drifted closer over to the other side of the lake. The policeman was looking down at them from the bridge that separated the lake's end from the river leading to Birchwood town docks.

He cleared his throat. "Well, Mr. Fuller, I don't know how you got here with Miss Henley—Lydie, that is you, isn't it?" .

"Yes," she said meekly.

"I'm tempted to serve you with a citation," Kolker went on dryly. "We do have laws around here about public indecency, you know. But out of respect for Elly—that's Lydie's mother, young man—I'm going to look the other way, this once."

"I appreciate that, sir," said Justin.

"I happen to be an early riser," Kolker said. "But if you make good time, you should be able to paddle yourselves out of here before the whole of Birchwood becomes aware of your presence."

"Thank you," Justin said, already starting to move the raft while he still protected Lydie from the policeman's view.

"See you at the barbecue, Lydie," Kolker called.

"Okay, Mr. Kolker. Thanks a lot."

Only when Lydie could see the shoreline gliding by at a decent clip did she gently ease herself out from her protector, shivering with embarrassment in the early-morning light. As Justin chuckled, paddling with both hands, she couldn't help giggling herself.

"Nice fellow," Justin commented.

"Old friend of the family," she said, leaning over to add her hands to his in the cool water.

"Discreet?"

"I wouldn't count on it," she said ruefully. "As a matter of fact, I think you and I are about to make the local papers."

"Papers?" He looked at her, startled.

"Andy's brother runs the *Enterprise*," she sighed. "They haven't done a piece on you in the 'New Arrivals in Town' column yet—but I think you've just arrived."

"Ouch," Justin muttered, and paddled with renewed fervor. "Let's make tracks."

The sky was already pink with the approaching sunrise. It didn't take them long to get back to the corner of the lake where the cabin resided. Not another soul was visible along the distant shoreline.

Lydie was already reconciled to having made a public spectacle of herself, but her arms ached with exhaustion from the paddling as they eased the raft back into the boathouse. Her stomach growled with hunger.

"Do you really know how to make French toast?" she asked as he lifted her up onto the dock.

"Do we really know how to get ourselves into trouble?" he countered, grinning, and leaned forward to kiss her wetly as she laughed.

Her laughter died as he kissed her with more urgency, and the passion she always felt when he touched her flared anew. His lips were sweet, tasting of fresh lake water, and his skin smelled wonderfully of his natural scent mixed with her own.

"I really do need some breakfast," she murmured as he nibbled at her lip, his hands finding the softness of her breasts and cradling them gently.

"Here's a delicious appetizer...," he answered, then deepened the kiss, his tongue seeking hers.

"Justin..." She had come up for air, her breath coming in a ragged gasp. "There *are* people living on this lake. Officer Kolker won't pass up that citation a second time."

Justin looked around him as if aware of their now-sunlit nudity for the first time. "Breakfast, then," he muttered. "Inside."

Taking her hand, he swung himself up onto the dock. Then, arm in arm, they walked back to the cabin. Her marigolds and morning glories were glimmering in the rosy dawnlight as they approached. She felt like Eve in the garden.

"What was that about a barbecue?" he asked.

"It's the Labor Day celebration," she said. "The locals always cook up a storm when the summer people leave."

"Sounds like fun," he said. "Think I might qualify as an honorary local? Because, Lydie..." He turned her to face him at the bottom of the steps. "I'm not ready to leave."

A little shiver of happiness ran through her as she looked into the warmth of his dark eyes. Just as quickly, she felt a chill of anxiety. Would the happiness last?

Doubts and fears hovered like phantoms, but they were already evaporating with the morning mist when he squeezed her hand, and an answering warmth rose from deep within her. "That's good," she said, no longer feeling any shyness as she stood before him in the morning light. "Because, fool that I am, I probably wouldn't let you go."

CHAPTER THIRTEEN

IT TOOK THREE of them to carry the huge wooden bowl to the picnic table—Lydie, Julie Wendkos, and Nan O'Byrne, who mainly ran interference. People kept grabbing radishes, carrots, or bits of lettuce out of it as they walked, and with the children underfoot and the general pandemonium on all sides, just getting the salad to its rightful destination was like running on obstacle course.

The table was already laden with other salads, this one end to end with another, and another beyond that. The air was thick with the smell of wood burning and charcoal from the pit nearby, where practically an entire cow was roasting, and the woods were alive with the sound of rhythm and blues.

Jason Polhamus and His Blue Ball Busters—best of the local bands—were set up on a platform at the edge of the clearing, tearing into a raucous shuffle. People moved to the beat wherever they stood, some of the teenagers spontaneously grabbing hold of partners, then careening off into their own laughing orbits, pulling friends and older folks along.

Lydie, narrowly avoiding a collision with one such red-faced couple, scanned the crowd looking for Justin. He'd been carried off by her father and Grandpa to take part in the infamous Perry Dunklow Invitational Golf Tournament. That particular sporting event—more an excuse for the men of Birchwood to consume massive quantities of beer while they gleefully destroyed the local golf course—should have been over by now.

Lydie caught sight of her father, the fire chief, and Larry from the bait shop setting up a card table amid the larch trees. She hurried over, snaking through the throngs of people, and reached the men as they were sitting down for what was bound to be a marathon poker game.

"Hey, it's Lydie of the Lake," the fire chief boomed as her father gave her a welcoming hug.

"Enough of that," her father admonished his friend, noticing Lydie's blush at the salutation. News of her raft travels with Justin Fuller had spread quickly throughout the community, and she'd had to bear many a good-natured kidding that afternoon. But one comforting thought was that her own notorious brush with the law would undoubtedly be eclipsed by a myriad of other scandals before the night was through.

The annual Beef Roast was traditionally a time for age-old feuds to be rekindled, illicit romances to be consummated, and vandalism of all kinds to be perpetrated in the name of fun. Last summer, for example, according to the tales she'd heard, the Tanner twins had driven their father's Ford right off the dock and into the river in the midst of the revelries. From the look of things, this celebration would be as uproarious as any other.

"What have you done with Justin?" Lydie asked, ruffling her dad's hair. "Is he here?"

"Should be soon," he said. "Who's got the chips?"

More folding chairs were being pulled up to the table. Lydie knew that in a few minutes there wouldn't be any getting through to these men. The game usually got serious before sundown. In one such poker marathon, the Henleys' next-door neighbor had lost his shirt, his station wagon, and a horse, in that order, before the night was through.

"I don't see him," Lydie said impatiently. "You didn't leave him wandering around the golf course or something, did you?"

"No, he's got more sense than that," her dad scoffed. "Pretty handy with a nine-iron, too."

"He had a hot date," Larry said, winking at her as he piled up some red chips.

"Don't listen to 'em," Mr. Henley said. "He did say something about a phone call, though."

"I think we should make room for a beer keg, right about here," one of the other men interrupted, and Lydie walked off, exasperated. Mrs. Henley was helping another woman load a giant screen with corn in the husks, and Lydie pitched in, her eyes still searching for a glimpse of Justin in the crowd.

She'd be having a better time if he were at her side. The fact that she couldn't enjoy the fun without him worried her even more. Was she already that far gone? Lost without him, overnight, just when she'd spent months trying to regain a sense of independence?

Nonsense. But if he ended up shut up with his

computer and phone on a night like this...

She was watching the roast being carved up, the sun beginning to set over the hill, when strong hands grabbed her around the waist and hoisted her suddenly into the air. "Justin!" she cried as he whirled her around to face him.

"Sorry I'm late," he murmured, letting her down and pulling her close. As he kissed her, she inhaled the scent of him, the taste of him bringing back deliciously erotic memories, the feel of his body against hers the headiest of aphrodisiacs.

When his lips left hers, they gazed at each other for a moment, inhabiting a circle of quiet intensity like the eye of a hurricane. She could see that a fresh tan was deepening his color. His face was sexily unshaven, his hair unkempt, his dark eyes gleaming with an enjoyment of her, of the night, of life.

"You look happy," she said as his lips brushed her cheek.

"I am. We've made some headway. The chemical composition of the chip coat—" He stopped himself, shaking his head with a sheepish smile. "I'll spare you the details."

"You mean you're not just happy to see me?" she teased with a mock pout.

"But that's why," he protested. "I can leave the next few test runs to the boys in the lab, and put the whole problem out of my mind for tonight. From now until dawn it's just you and me."

They both laughed as an exuberant pair of kids raced each other around them, followed by a barking dog, and the sound of electric guitars tuning up again added to the general melee.

"Just the two of us," she said wryly. "How did you like the golf game?"

"Game?" He took her hand and led her through the crowd of revelers in the direction of the roast. "I've never played much golf—but even *I* know that's not how it's supposed to be done."

"I believe the general idea is to chase each other around in those little carts and destroy the course, isn't it?"

Justin nodded, chuckling. "That was it." They had joined the informal line of people gathered now, paper plates in hand, around the pit where the giant roast was being carved. Lydie introduced Justin to one person after another—although from their sly references to the morning's rafting, a few seemed to know who he was already.

Lydie was glad to see Justin welcomed by her Birchwood friends, including Marge, the taxi dispatcher, who was visiting from Traverse City. Marge, seeing Lydie enjoying the company of the tall, handsome Justin, couldn't resist giving her some arch I-told-you-so glances.

Balancing plates heaped with beef, salad, and corn, Lydie and Justin made their way into the woods, where other couples were picnicking in the twilight. They found a comfortable perch far enough away from the noisy clearing to be able to talk easily as they ate.

"It was really you that did it, you know," he said, pausing to butter his sweet corn. "By coaxing me into an open frame of mind. I'd been batting my head against an invisible wall, but being with you sort of scrambled all of my usual cognitive patterns—loosened me up. And just as I was stepping onto the green this afternoon with your grandfather, I got an entirely new angle on the problem with the chip."

"Do you think your cognitive patterns will get unscrambled again?" she asked with mock concern.

"Hopefully not," he said, affection gleaming in his eyes as he took her hand. "I'm enjoying being . . . discombobulated."

"Could be bad for you," she joked.

"Impossible," he said. "In fact, I may have to put you under contract." He kissed her fingertips, and her skin tingled at the gentle, moist touch of his lips.

"No way," she murmured, feeling a tremble of desire as he kissed his way from the base of her thumb to palm and wrist. "I'm a free-lancer now."

"We'll see about that . . . ," he said, pulling her close.

Of course she didn't take it seriously, their playful banter. How could she expect either of them to think about the future? She was doing her best to take it as it came, enjoying the time they had together.

When the band struck up a slow country ballad, Justin took Lydie by the hand, and they moved from the trees to the edge of the clearing, where couples old and young were moving slowly to the sweet sounds of guitar and pedal steel. She settled into the soft, secure contours of his warm arms and let the music flow around and through her.

For someone who, she assumed, was not famed as a rug-cutter, Justin proved to be graceful on his feet. She was able to follow his every move as easily as if they had always danced like this. She could feel his strong thighs pressing against hers through the thin material of her white lace skirt, and a warm tenuril of arousal rose in her loins as he held her even closer.

molding her body to his.

"You waltz pretty well for a mad scientist," she said.

"And I suppose you give tap lessons on alternate Thursdays, among your fifty professions," he murmured, nuzzling her ear as he guided her fluidly through the dancing couples.

"Ballet," she sighed. She closed her eyes, leaning back in his embrace, dimly aware that the music was ending but enjoying the floating feeling too much to want to stop. They swayed together in the warm silence, listening only to the music of each other's heartbeat, until at last they broke apart, smiling at their own enrapturement.

"Thirsty?" Justin asked, and Lydie nodded. "I'll get us some fresh drinks," he said, letting go of her slowly, savoring each moment of their embrace. Lydie watched him move off through the darkness, his tall figure illuminated now as the bonfire on the hilltop was ignited.

It wasn't love, she told herself, knowing that she lied but hardly caring. She sauntered toward the rising flames of the bonfire, feeling a blissful light-headedness that was sweeter than any wine's inebriation.

Jimmy, the White Finch bartender, was one of a group gathered at the periphery of the blaze. Dateless, he made his usual teasing play for her, and she laughed him off good-naturedly, accepting his friendly hug with a minimum of protest.

Fortunately, Justin wasn't in the vicinity. Not that he was necessarily the jealous type, she reminded herself—though she secretly hoped he was. But then, where was he?

Realizing he'd been gone much longer than he

should have to get a few glasses of soda, Lydie left the bonfire and strolled over to the picnic tables. There was a small crowd gathered around one, and as soon as she saw it, she somehow sensed she'd found her man.

She wasn't entirely prepared for the spectacle that greeted her. Justin had lined up a dozen wineglasses, each filled with a different amount of apple cider. With an expression of intense concentration, he was treating his delighted audience to a glass-harmonica rendition of "Home on the Range."

As Justin played the glass tops with nimble fingers moving over the vibrating edges, each glass sending out an airy but perfectly tuned tone, Jason Polhamus joined in an acoustic guitar, and before long all the onlookers were singing, Lydie included.

A grin of bashful pleasure lit Justin's face as his eyes found Lydie's in the crowd. Then, red-faced in the firelight, he gave a helpless shrug as, spurred on by applause, he led them through a spirited performance of "She'll Be Coming Round the Mountain."

"Your days as a fudgie are officially over," Lydie told him hours later, when they rocked in the rope hammock outside the cabin by the lake.

"I've passed the tests?" He kissed her forehead, rocking them gently in the warm breeze.

"Umm," she murmured. "You couldn't pass for a city slicker now if you tried." She could feel every inch of her vibrate softly as he held her close, and she stretched like a kitten against him, enjoying his little sigh of arousal as she slid along his body.

"You people certainly know how to celebrate the end of summer," he said. His lips found the soft curve of her neck, kissing a warm, satiny path along the tender skin. Lydie arched her back as desire blossomed inside of her.

"You mean running amok?" she murmured. "You were the life of the party yourself," she reminded him. Justin's impromptu show might have gone on for hours if she hadn't spirited him away.

"I guess I've never felt so . . . alive," he whispered. His lips were moving down the deep V of her oversized knit sweater, his hands deftly sliding up her bare stomach with caresses that made her tremble.

"Not bad for a . . . former misfit," she teased him.

"You're right," he said softly. "I've been fitting in. Not just with this place, but fitting with you."

"I like the way I fit you," she whispered. Then her breath caught in her throat as his hand found the naked skin of her breast and he cupped the soft globe of flesh in his smooth palm. As he kneaded its stiffening tip, his lips claimed hers again.

She felt herself unfurling like the petals of a hothouse flower, moist with inflamed arousal. Their kiss deepened, and she was awash in voluptuous sensations, her hands roving eagerly over his body as he caressed hers in the swaying hammock.

"Lydie," he murmured when they broke apart, "I don't know if this is safe, but I'm getting a wild idea . . ."

She smiled, gazing into the depths of his dark eyes. The slow rocking of the hammock lent a dizzying sensation that only seemed to add to their arousal. "I like the way you think," she whispered. "Don't worry. It's only a few feet to the ground."

With a deep-throated chuckle, he kissed her again, his tongue seeking hers in the warm, wet cavern of her mouth. Her hands roved eagerly beneath the band of his trousers, seeking his aroused flesh as he sought hers.

Soon their clothes were crumpled around their feet, Lydie's lace skirt a sheet beneath them, as the hammock swayed. Justin pulled her against his hard, hot length, murmuring her name. She wound her fingers in his hair, relishing the feel of his nakedness entwined with hers.

The yearning to feel possessed by him overpowered her, and she moved sinuously against him, returning his urgent kisses and caresses. This time their union was one of kindred spirits, a slow melding of two lovers who had learned already how to give and take the most, the best, the sweetest pleasures they could share. They coaxed each other to one joyful fulfillment after another, suspended weightless above the world, lost in the loving of each other through an endless, star-filled night.

Vermilion red splashed against a cobalt blue. Shimmering yellow flecks, sprayed across a swath of deeper oranges, glowed star bright as her brush hovered above the canvas.

Lydie paused, then pounced, her hand moving swiftly, the brush end swirling, darting here and there as if it had a life of its own. She didn't stop to think, to measure any move, but merely felt, letting the feelings propel her, the colors guide her.

She was cresting on a wave of exhilaration she hadn't felt in the longest time—a rushing burst of sensation that filled and emptied her, again and again, like a tide building and ebbing without end. It was like . . .

. . . making love, she realized when she stopped to catch her breath some time later. Radiant with excitement, she looked down at the sprawling, glowing canvas. As her mind filled again with images of the night before, she knew what was inspiring this outburst of ecstatic color.

Flushed and breathless, Lydie put the brush down. Being with Justin had been like this, she mused, squinting at the painting now with a more analytic eye. She'd been trying to express it—that ever-cresting joy she'd felt in his arms, that reaching for the highest peak and sailing past it she'd experienced when his heart and hers had beat as one.

She couldn't help her smile of pride as she beheld this thing that had practically leaped out of her full-blown. Her first impulse was to gather it up, still wet, run the mile down the road to the man who'd symbolically fathered it, and thrust it into his arms.

But, no—she'd have to wait. She'd be seeing him in just a few hours, and she knew he was immersed in his own work now. It wouldn't be fair to burst in on him like that, tempting as it seemed.

Lydie exhaled a deep breath and stepped back from the easel. Looking down at herself, she let out a peal of laughter. There was nearly as much color on her pants, smock, sneakers, and hands as there was on the canvas. She was suddenly so light-headedly happy she could have sung.

Fool! she silently chided herself, taking another step back, still unable to keep from looking at the gleaming canvas in the quiet little room upstairs at the Henleys'. Why did you wait so long? What could you have been afraid of?

She'd forgotten how good it felt, just painting for

the sheer fun of it and nothing else. All that time in New York she'd spent worrying, comparing, competing had nearly wiped out the memory. But *he'd* helped bring it back, she thought, and a wave of love spiraled up inside her again like a restless fever.

This was crazy. She was six times a fool to let herself moon over the man, to let herself go like this. And fool that she was, Lydie found herself flying down the stairs, sending terrified rabbits and birds scattering in her wake. She careened into the kitchen, nearly causing her mother to drop the bowl of egg whites she was beating, and dialed the phone at the speed of light.

If she couldn't see him, she could talk to him at least—just for a moment, to let him know. She wanted to thank him for saying what he had, for doing what he'd done. She hadn't told him how much she loved him—not in those words. And such an absurd omission struck her now as criminal.

Mrs. Henley stood behind her at the counter, shaking her head with a rueful smile as she returned to her egg whites. "You did spread newspapers down, dear?" she queried gently as Lydie paced restlessly in a small circle, then stopped short, crestfallen.

The line was busy.

She should have known. Lydie shrugged, and put the receiver back in its cradle. "What, Mom?"

"Newspapers, Lydie. You look as though you just danced through a paint factory, and I was only hoping..."

"Of course I did," Lydie assured her. She gave her mother an affectionate peck on the cheek. "And I'll clean up, don't worry," she called over her shoulder, heading back upstairs again.

Even though it should have been only a minor disappointment, Lydie couldn't help but feel a moment had been lost, a moment that mattered. She'd wanted Justin to share this with her. With a sigh, she strode back into the room and hurried to the easel for another look.

Hmm.

Lydie's eyes narrowed. The painting still glimmered and shone, still seemed to sing with feeling, but now first doubts hovered around her as she gave it a critical once-over. It was messy, sloppy, perhaps overrun with movement. It was...

"Unprofessional," whispered an old demon in her ear. "Not as good as...," sighed another. "Too personal," sniggered a third ghostly critic. And yet one more hissed:

"What if he hates it?"

Lydie shook her head, wanting to silence them all. For a second she succeeded, and she heard herself— or was it Justin?—saying, "Let it be, Lydie. It's just ... you."

But then, as she looked, and looked again, she could see room for improvements. Certainly a few little touch-ups couldn't hurt. Lydie regarded the easel with a practiced eye.

She wasn't due at the cabin for a while. In the meantime, she'd see if she could, well, clean the thing up a bit. With a grimace of determination, she rolled back her sleeves and picked up the paintbrush once more.

CHAPTER FOURTEEN

LYDIE PAUSED AT the screen door, a little out of breath. She raised her fist, about to knock, then stopped herself, peering inside.

Of course—what had she been thinking of? She'd rushed like a madwoman to scrub the paint off, shower, wash her hair, get dressed, and get here at the stroke of eight—well, only a few minutes late. They had reservations at the Fisherman's Inn in Larchwood, a fancy restaurant in a neighboring town, and since it was to be their most formal date so far, she'd wanted to be ready on time.

But Justin Fuller was sitting at his computer, telephone at his ear, still wearing the pair of jeans and T-shirt she'd left him in that morning—still in practically the same position, for Pete's sake!

Lydie sighed and opened the door, being careful not to scrape the edge of the canvas on the doorframe as she entered. She rested it gently against the table near Justin and then came up behind him, sliding her hands around his waist.

"Calibrations still don't check out," he was saying into the telephone, his fingers darting over the keyboard in his lap. As he felt Lydie's embrace, he stiffened slightly, startled, then relaxed and leaned back in his chair to nuzzle her neck with a warm, wet kiss.

Somewhat mollified, she ruffled his hair, then sat in the chair to his side and waited patiently for him to wrap things up. She saw, with a vague sense of foreboding, that he was knee-deep in computer printout spreadsheets and wore an expression that was far from relaxed.

Restless, she got up and paced around behind him, then seized the painting. She spent a few minutes propping it up properly to catch the light from the lamp on the table, and by the time she was done, miraculously, Justin was getting off the phone.

"Hey, good-lookin'," he murmured, straightening up with a little wince as obviously stiff muscles made their complaints known.

Lydie went to him. Her arms slid around his neck as she welcomed him with a warm and provocative kiss. He tasted good. He felt good. It was all coming back to her fast. And Justin savored the taste and feel of her, too, with a husky sound of pleasure coming from deep in his throat.

When the mist of passion that clouded her eyes finally faded, and his lips left hers, Lydie gazed up into his dark, velvet eyes, trying to recapture the feeling of annoyance she'd been having moments earlier, but it wasn't easy.

Justin cleared his throat. "Now, Lydie, don't get upset," he began, "but I'm not going to be ready to go for a while."

The annoyance returned with lightning speed. "Jus-

tin," she groaned. "Tonight? You have to work tonight?"

"I'm as unhappy about it as you are," he sighed.
"But we're still trying to work out this chip problem.
I've had the guys at the plant working through Labor
Day on it," he added pointedly as she started to move
away. "So if I have to be late for dinner . . ."

"I know, I know," she muttered. "Here's the part
where I'm supposed to be marvelously understanding."

"It would help," he agreed with a faint smile.

"I'll give it a try," she said. Then the reason for
her initial jubilation came back to her. "Justin! You
can take a one-minute break, can't you?"

He cast an anxious glance at his computer and the
phone next to it, but he nodded nonetheless. "Of
course."

Lydie took his hand and led him over to the table.
She stepped back, holding her breath as Justin stood
stock-still, gazing at the canvas in silence. But after
a few moments, she couldn't contain herself. "What
do you think?"

"When did you do this?" he asked. His voice
sounded pleased, but certainly too noncommittal for
her taste.

"Just hours ago. So what do you think?"

"It's beautiful," he said.

"You really think so?" Lydie stood next to him,
lips pursed, trying to see the canvas through his eyes.
When she'd gone back to work on it, she'd smoothed
out the rough edges, cleaned up areas that she'd been
afraid were too violently colorful. Her only worry was
that she might have gone too far.

"Yes," Justin murmured, leaning forward to peer

more closely at the surface of the painting. "I like it."

Lydie knew she could be oversensitive, but his reaction still troubled her. Like? He was supposed to love it! And she had the feeling he was editing his response.

"What's it called?" he asked.

Lydie cleared her throat. *"Hammock Swirl,"* she said. "Of course, that's just a working title."

Justin looked over his shoulder at her, amusement glinting in his eyes. "Interesting name," he murmured, then returned to his close inspection.

"You don't really like it," she said.

"No, I do," he said, then straightened up. "But..."

"But what?" she demanded.

Justin shook his head at her evident anxiety. "Lydie, it's wonderful," he said. "And I can't tell you how exciting it is to see you working again—"

"But?" she prompted, her pulse pounding.

Justin frowned. "Nothing," he muttered. "The colors are amazing. Are you happy with it?"

"You're not telling me what you think," she said stubbornly, folding her arms. "Out with it, Justin Fuller."

Justin looked from her to the painting and then back again, seeming to weigh his response. "Well," he said cautiously, "it looks like parts of it have been painted over a bit."

"Overpainted?"

"No, I mean—"

"I know what you mean." Lydie frowned. "I did go back and redo some things," she admitted, feeling a tightness take hold of her that started at her throat and spread to clench the rest of her body.

Justin was nodding thoughtfully. "Why?"

"Why?" she repeated.

Why, she wondered, was she being so defensive? He was right—she knew what he was getting at even before he said it, and she knew instinctively the mistake she'd made. But owning up to it seemed much too painful.

"You had second thoughts, didn't you?" he suggested quietly.

Lydie shrugged, her heart racing.

"I can see the first impulse there on the canvas," he went on, "and it's quite amazing—intense, unique, even daring." Enthusiasm vibrated in his voice as he gestured at the canvas. Then he gazed at her, and she could see a glimmer of disappointment in his eyes. "You had it," he said gently. "But then... you got cold feet, Lydie. You tried to cover it up—cover yourself up."

Lydie stared at him, lips set tight. Why did he have to be so damned perceptive? She was searching for a suitable defense, some reply to justify her actions, when the phone rang. Lydie whirled to look at it, wishing it would disintegrate before ringing again.

Justin made an apologetic gesture and moved past her to answer it. *Don't!* she nearly yelled, but she stood, frozen, as he reached down and picked up the receiver on its second ring. "Yes? Right, I still have it on my screen..."

He looked at her, miming exasperation as he listened. Lydie stood where she was, her emotions churning. She suddenly felt like a reprimanded child who'd come running over with her latest mud pie, only to be told it was... mud.

"Jeff, can you hold on a moment?" Justin covered the mouthpiece. "Lydie, I'm really sorry, but I do have to take this call. You understand, don't you? I'll be with you as soon as I can."

She understood. As Justin returned to his conversation, she watched him take his seat before the screen, watched him start to type again as he talked. He was already light-years away from her, dealing with equations and calibrations that meant millions of dollars and would affect millions of people.

What made her think she could be as important? What was a three-by-two canvas smeared with oils, next to a minuscule microchip coveted by the Pentagon? And as for a seafood dinner at the Fisherman's Inn, here in the wilds of Nowhere, U.S.A.—what did that matter?

Lydie walked stiffly to the table. She took the canvas down and headed for the door. She paused there, staring at the back of Justin's head, willing him to turn around. But he didn't. He was utterly engrossed in his computer screen, and she didn't exist.

It wasn't until the door had slammed behind her and she had hurried to the car, practically throwing the canvas into the back seat, that Lydie realized how much she'd secretly counted on his getting up, following her, trying to stop her. But he hadn't.

So here she was, all dressed up with nowhere to go. Lydie gunned her motor and pulled down the driveway with a screech of tires. She reached for the windshield wipers before she realized it was her eyes that were shimmering with wet tears; the sky was perfectly clear. Radio blasting till her speakers rattled, Lydie spun around the turn and headed into town.

Jimmy had wanted to drive her home, which was a perfectly ridiculous idea, Lydie mused. She was cruising down the highway at a sedate speed, and there was absolutely nothing wrong with her driving prowess.

Birchwood had been dead when she'd zoomed in—how many hours earlier she wasn't sure. The day after the Beef Roast was traditionally one that just about everybody slept through, anyway, so everything had been closed.

Even the White Finch was desolate when she'd strolled in. Jimmy hadn't been behind the bar, but at the pay phone. The place was deserted, and Willy was in the process of turning out lights. When Lydie poured herself a stiff shot and a beer back, Willy hadn't said a word, of course, but Jimmy took notice.

Apparently he'd been in the midst of setting up a Hangover Party at his friend Luke Gleason's place, some twenty miles away in Maple City. So of course he'd extended an invite, and Lydie had been happy to take him up on it.

There were lots of people there from Birchwood, some she hadn't had a real conversation with in years. She played some darts, even joined the men in some moonlit target practice out back, and boy, did it feel good to fire off a few rounds, even if they were only BBs.

Jimmy, ever optimistic, had done his best to make her warm up to him, and she felt a twinge of guilt when she put him off, as she always did. Even if she'd been interested, in her heart it would have felt like infidelity—not that she was in a relationship that required fidelity.

After all, she mused woozily, approaching the Henley homestead, she was in love with a man who was faithful to his computer first. Lydie sighed, as she'd been sighing at various points throughout this evening of good times that just hadn't been all that good. How did she get herself mixed up with these men? Hadn't she learned anything?

She braked suddenly and peered through the windshield, disoriented. There was another car in the driveway, blocking hers. That was odd. But she wasn't going to waste any time worrying about it. She had an appointment with a couple of rabbits and a nice soft bed.

She climbed out of the car, grabbed the canvas from the back seat, shut the car door with exaggerated quietness—no need to wake up the household at this hour—and walked up the path to the front porch.

For no explicable reason, she was humming "She'll Be Coming Round the Mountain," but almost at the porch steps, she stopped, the song dying on her lips. A figure had risen out of the darkness on the porch, and a voice that didn't sound particularly relaxed rose with it.

"Where in heaven's name have you been?"

Lydie frowned, staring up at Justin Fuller. What was he looking so hot and bothered about? "Out," she muttered. "You mind?"

He was down the steps now, striding up to her with eyes blazing. Justin took hold of her by the shoulders with a not-so-gentle grip. "You're all right?" he said, his voice a tense growl.

"Course I'm all right," she said, trying to move out of his grasp. That wasn't an easy task. Her canvas thumped to the grass behind her, but she couldn't even twist away to pick it up.

"Where were you?" he demanded. Lydie swal-

lowed, her slightly tipsy devil-may-care feeling evaporating. She'd never seen Justin Fuller angry. She was
suddenly quite certain it wasn't a sight she wanted to
see again.

"I was somewhere in Hicksville," she said de-
fiantly. "Playing with the local colors, so to speak."

Justin swore softly under his breath and abruptly
let her go. Lydie nearly lost her balance and stumbled
slightly, but she straightened up in a hurry. Justin was
kicking at imaginary rocks and continuing a whispered
litany of curses.

Even though there was something fearful about his
wrath, she didn't quite understand it. What did *he*
have to be angry about? She was the one who'd been
left high and dry after having her labor of love so
casually dismissed. Lydie cleared her throat.

"I'd like to go in now," she said politely, and bent
to pick up her canvas.

"How could you do this?" He was facing her again,
jaw tight, brow furrowed, eyes radiating fire and brim-
stone.

"How could I? It was easy. Well, for heaven's sake,
Justin," she said, taking a step back as he glowered
more fiercely at her. "You were busy with your phone
and your chip and everything—I wasn't about to have
my dinner at breakfast."

"You might have waited."

"You might have taken a few more minutes to talk
to me," she said evenly.

"Or told me where you were going," he added.

"I didn't know where I was going," she exclaimed,
her anger mounting. "And since when do I have to
tell you about every move I make?"

Justin was silent a moment, merely glaring at her. When he spoke again, it was obvious it took a lot of effort to keep his voice as low and steady as he did. "I drove," he said, with exaggerated calm, "from here to Glen Lake looking for you. I drove around the shore of Lake Michigan and back. I've been down every road in this town and half the roads in this state for the past four or five hours!"

Lydie shook her head. "I don't see why you—"

"I even got Officer Kolker involved," he went on. "Not that he was much help. Apparently, all of your local buddies wouldn't lose any sleep if you fell off the edge of the earth when they weren't looking. Even your family assumed you were perfectly okay—"

"And why shouldn't they?" she protested. "Justin, I'm a big girl! I took care of myself without any difficulty before I met you, and I'm sure I'll take care of myself fine after you leave!"

That shut him up. Justin shoved his hands in his pockets, lips set tight, and turned away again. Lydie stared at him, befuddled. In a way, she felt flattered that he'd spent all that time looking for her. In a way, it served him right. But she still couldn't entirely fathom the reason for his being so concerned.

"Don't you think you're overreacting?" she said.

Justin whipped around as if he'd been hit. *"I'm* overreacting? Look at you—running out on me like that just because I had to deal with a phone call."

"Which was obviously more important than me or my feelings!" she shot back. "You know how much it meant to me, doing this." She brandished the canvas at him. "And after blithely informing me that it wasn't any good, you return to your—"

"I never said that," he retorted. "You know I didn't. Maybe you didn't want to hear what I really did say, but that's not..." His voice trailed off as he stared at the painting in her hand. "What did you do to it?" he asked, eyes widening.

"I gave it some more rough edges," she said dryly. When Luke and friends had run out of bottles and cans to shoot at, Lydie had volunteered the canvas, which now sported a number of holes in an asymmetrical pattern. It had seemed like a good idea at the time, but now, as his eyes left the canvas to gaze at her with an expression that made her wince inwardly, it was beginning to seem foolish.

"You little... idiot," he said softly, shaking his head.

"Yes, I'm an idiot," she returned, her anger flaring up again. "I'm an idiot for thinking that I could get involved with you for more than a day. It's not that I'm blaming you, Justin—you never promised me anything more. It's my fault for getting carried away."

"Don't say that!" His face was ashen. "You know you mean more to me than that. We *are* involved— and being involved means you can't just run off like that and think it doesn't matter! You can't go flying around, heedless of the consequences—"

"But you can," she reminded him hotly. "You can have planes fly you here and there at a moment's notice. You can be here and then gone, for all I know! And even when you're here, it's your work that takes priority. Why shouldn't it?" she added bitterly.

"That's not how I want it to be," he exclaimed. "I want it to be you and me, together—"

"But you should know better." She sighed. "Didn't

you say yourself that you and relationships don't mix? And the irony is, I've said the same thing about myself!"

"You're being irrational," he said sharply. "If you'd only—"

"No, I'm being rational," she cried. "That's just it. You're the one going berserk just because I—I happened to go off and have a good time when you didn't have the time to have a good time with me."

"You shouldn't have done it!" he exploded. "You have no idea what it felt like, being worried sick that something had happened."

"All that happened is that I got wise!" she snapped. "I came to my senses. And you seem to have lost yours altogether," she added, stepping past him. "Honestly, Justin, you may need a keeper, but I certainly don't!"

She strode quickly up the steps, the canvas flapping against her legs. She was suddenly exhausted, tired of the whole messy, hurtful situation. This was too much like the fights she'd had with Martin, even though the ache she felt in her heart seemed worse. She didn't want to talk things out. She wanted out, period.

"Lydie..."

Lydie paused and turned back to face him, her hand on the doorknob. "Justin, maybe we just shouldn't see each other," she said, her voice unnaturally stiff, barely her own. "I don't think this... being together is good for either of us."

Justin stared up at her, his expression unfathomable. Was it pain or anger that flashed in the depths of his dark eyes? She couldn't see, and wasn't sure she wanted to. Calm as she might have sounded, she was running scared. She couldn't go through it all again...

"If that's what you want." His voice was low and pained in the darkness behind her. She was tempted to stop, to go back and try to understand...

But understanding how things were wouldn't make her feel any better about it. "Good-bye, Justin," she murmured, and she hurriedly opened the door and escaped into the safety of the house.

She chanced one glance through the curtained glass, but the sight of Justin standing where she'd left him, staring up at the shut door with a pained look on his face, only gave her insides a wrench.

Lydie turned away. She didn't want to feel guilty. She just wanted to go to sleep.

CHAPTER FIFTEEN

"LYDIE?"

Lydie looked up from the table, glanced at the proffered piece of pie, and shook her head. "No, thanks," she said, and returned to a perusal of her glass. It was one of the finest of her mother's glass collection, a miniature Leaning Tower of Pisa. At the moment it was filled with water, and spilling not a drop.

How did they do it? she wondered absently, then looked up again, aware of a pregnant silence in the room.

Her father was looking at her oddly, as was Aunt Helen, to his left. Lydie turned toward Grandpa, and saw him exchanging a glance with her mother, who merely shook her head, then looked down at her plate.

"Sorry," Lydie said, perplexed. "Did I miss something?"

No one answered her. Instead, Grandpa leaned forward, addressing her father *sotto voce:* "It's worse than we thought."

Her father nodded unhappily. "So it seems."

Silence reigned again, as all the other members of the family began to eat their respective pieces of pie with a notable lack of enthusiasm. Lydie cleared her throat.

"Excuse me," she said. "But what is it?"

Grandpa fixed her with a sorrowful gaze, taking a forkful of pie, then chewing thoughtfully. "Your mother probably doesn't want us making a big deal out of it," he said at length. "But it is pretty upsetting."

"Now, Dad," Mrs. Henley said. "There's no need—"

"Well, it's history," he mumbled, and then was silent.

"Would somebody please—" Lydie began.

"You didn't eat it," piped up Aunt Helen, who then covered her mouth discreetly with her napkin.

"You passed up a piece of Mom's strawberry-rhubarb pie," her father said gently. "That seems to be a first."

Lydie looked at the faces around the table. She didn't know whether to laugh or cry. Instead, she blushed deeply and wished she could somehow disappear.

She'd been a holy mess for days—cranky at breakfast, morose at lunch, nearly comatose at dinner. The day before yesterday she'd snapped at Aunt Helen and taken a swipe at her parrot. Yesterday she'd burst into tears when Grandpa offered to treat her to a movie in Traverse City. She'd spent practically this entire day shut up in her room.

But through it all, nobody had complained, taken offense, or demanded explanations. It was so like the Henleys. Only now, when she refused a piece of pie, did they show their true concern.

She could understand it, in a way, considering her mother's strawberry-rhubarb pie was probably Lydie's favorite food in the universe. At the age of six, she'd made herself horribly sick sneaking downstairs in the middle of the night to finish off a half of one by herself. And every time she'd had it since, when living at home or visiting, she could be counted on to devour at least two or three slices.

Come to think of it, her mother had probably baked this one in an attempt to cheer her up. That thought was enough to make tears well in Lydie's eyes. She rose from her chair, hurried over to her mother, and got in a hug and a quick peck on the kindly woman's cheek before the tears burst forth in earnest.

Then she ran from the room and up the stairs, Scruff barking at her heels. Once inside her room, she shut the door and bawled into her pillow.

After she'd snuffled her way through another mound of tissues, Lydie walked listlessly to the window and looked out at the darkened yard. Scruff stood at her side, a slipper raised hopefully in his teeth.

"You, too?" she said, smiling at the dog's attempt to enliven the situation. "No, thanks." She petted Scruff and returned to her examination of the treetops, trying not to remember that somewhere on the other side of them was a cabin with a man in it, a cabin she could see from here if a mile or so of woods were to magically disappear.

Scruff was nudging her leg with another object. Lydie looked down, and this time had to admire the dog's inventiveness. He was offering her a paintbrush that he'd found on the floor.

"Actually, that's not a bad idea," she murmured,

taking the brush from between his teeth. As Scruff looked on, tail wagging with interest, she spread newspapers on the floor and set up the easel again in front of the window.

If she was going to spend the evening shut up here—and she couldn't imagine doing anything else in her current state of mind—she might as well be productive. So what if nobody else appreciated her work? It gave *her* a good feeling, and that was the main thing, wasn't it?

Lydie felt her spirits lifting—well, perhaps an inch or two. She wouldn't cry it out, she'd paint it out. Blue period, indeed . . .

"Lydie, it's not that simple."

Lydie frowned at the speaker on her dashboard. "Sure it is," she said into the little microphone as she steered with care around a gargantuan pothole on Route 22. "Things just didn't work out, is all."

"You mean, *you* didn't work them out," Marge said. "You could have, you know."

Lydie sighed. "So what if I didn't want to?" She pulled the visor of her baseball cap down over her eyes. "And has he been banging down my door? Ringing the phone off the hook? No. Probably he's got his head stuck in a computer," she muttered. "Look, I'm not saying it was entirely his fault—"

"Doesn't sound like it was."

"I know I acted like a great big baby," Lydie admitted. "I shouldn't have reacted to his criticism like that. But, boy, he didn't have to blow up at me later like a crazy man."

"I only wish my Kenneth would give me that treatment when I come home late," Marge said. "Sounds to me like the man was just showing you how much he cares."

"I don't care how much he cares," said Lydie. "All right, I'll admit it—I just used the whole thing as an excuse. I wanted to get out, and I got out—before I could really hurt, you see?"

Marge's knowing chuckle ended in a crackle of static. "Sure. And now you're as happy as you can be."

Lydie was silent. She slowed for a squirrel that was standing in the middle of the road up ahead. Four days after Labor Day, and the stretch of highway that had been crammed with boat-toting cars full of tourists was as barren as Death Valley.

"Lydie," Marge said, "I haven't seen you this miserable since the first day you came back here. Remember? You were the sorriest bundle of broken heart bits I'd ever laid eyes on. Why, I had to get you this job just to give you a reason to live."

"For which I'm eternally grateful," Lydie said wryly.

"Well, if you ask me, getting involved with this Fuller fellow is the best thing that's happened to you since. And now you want to throw it all away."

"Wrong again, Marge," Lydie said. "I shouldn't have tangled with him in the first place. His life's busy enough as it is—and mine was just getting blissfully uncomplicated. Besides, who threw who away? He had to choose between me and a phone. Who got the nod?"

"From what I hear, Justin Fuller's been trying to run some pretty big-sized businesses long distance," Marge said. "You might want to cut him some slack."

Lydie glared at the speaker again, then sighed. "You're right," she muttered. "But the point is, I cut him loose altogether. And now we're both better off."

The radio was silent but for static. Lydie frowned. "Well, if you think I'm going to go back and try to work things out now, forget it. I've made enough of a fool of myself as it is."

"If you weren't the stubbornest Henley to come down the pike since your Grandma Estelle, I'd try to twist your arm," Marge said with a sigh. "But I guess it's too late anyway. Fuller's leaving town tomorrow."

"He is?" Lydie's heart gave a lurch. She struggled to regain her composure.

"According to John over at the airport, he's booked on a flight to Denver at sundown."

"That's just as well, then," Lydie said with forced calm.

"Uh-huh," drawled Marge. "Lydie, it's a good thing you never pursued a career on the stage. You couldn't act your way out of a paper bag."

"Thank you," Lydie said stiffly. "Give me a call if any fares come in." She shut off the radio, feeling a rush of anxiety and hopelessness. Well, that did it.

Or did it? As coincidence would have it, she was only a quarter mile from the turnoff to the cabin. Heart pounding, she considered the opportunity. Could she do it? Swallow her pride and try to make amends? All she had to do was steer a little to the left, and drive up that dirt road, and . . .

And nothing. Forget it, she told herself. Enough heartbreak for one year. She'd get over it, get on with her life.

Chicken, she murmured. And kept driving.

She wasn't sure how she'd been talked into it, but her mother had been unusually persuasive.

"It's for your father, really," Mrs. Henley had said. "He gets lonely on these trips."

"To Piker's Island?" Lydie asked, incredulous. "It's only an afternoon's worth of fishing. Why doesn't Grandpa go?"

"Grandpa's not feeling up to it. Humor him, dear," her mother had chided her. "If you do take that job in Los Angeles, he won't be seeing much of you for a while."

Lydie had been making phone calls, and one contact seemed to be coming through. It sounded promising—a job doing graphics for a small film company in Hollywood. It wasn't quite the fresh start she would have hoped for: it was even a step back, conceivably. But the Henleys had greeted the news with enthusiasm. Anything to make her happy, seemed to be the current of thought.

And so now, a little guilt had done the trick. Otherwise Lydie would never have found herself wading through the marshes, rod and reel in hand. She didn't mind a little casual fishing, but this wasn't quite her idea of a good time.

Lydie turned, frowning, looking for the figure of her father in the distance behind her. They'd barely gotten started, Mr. Henley waxing enthusiastic about the wonders of stalking coho salmon and steelhead trout, when he'd summarily abandoned her. He'd left some bait in the car.

Shrugging, she turned back, then smiled as she caught sight of her reflection in the water. This particular fashion trend would never catch on in Hollywood—a midriff-baring halter top over khaki shorts, with knee-high black rubber boots for wading.

Her father was certainly taking his sweet time.

Lydie listened for any movement in the tall grass. She thought she heard a car motor, which was odd. Finally, impatient and a little hot in the hazy late-afternoon sun, she started back toward the car.

She was already past the spot when she realized the car was gone. For a moment, she stood frozen, doubting her own memory. Hadn't it been parked right over that rise? Utterly confused, she began to walk farther on. Maybe she'd misjudged the distance.

Five, ten minutes later, she began to panic. It seemed she was completely lost. She was opening her mouth to give an existential yell into the surrounding wilderness, when she glimpsed someone through the trees that lined the beach.

"Hey!" she called, and she picked up speed, fumbling her way through the bushes growing in the ankle-deep water.

The fisherman—not her father, by the color of his clothes—turned in her direction, and then began walking toward her. Lydie slogged through the murky water, rounded a bend, and then stopped short, dropping her rod.

"Good grief," said Justin Fuller. "Don't tell me you're also a fishing guide."

CHAPTER SIXTEEN

IT CROSSED LYDIE'S mind that he looked about as at home on Piker's Island as a typewriter on a whale's back. Justin was dressed for concrete or carpet, omnipresent button-down shirt over wrinkled corduroys. His black loafers were soaked, and squeaked as he stepped closer, sweat beaded on his confused and reddened face.

For a moment, her heart throbbed with unbridled affection for the befuddled man. As he gazed at her, she thought she saw a flash of excited gladness in his eyes, but then he deliberately looked away from her, frowning.

"I seem to be a little lost," he muttered. "And you?"

"I was just . . . walking," she said lamely, adopting the same air of polite detachment.

They exchanged a quick, wary glance, and then simultaneously turned back in the directions from which they'd come. But this clearly struck them both as too ridiculous, because they immediately turned around again.

"How have you been?" he inquired with the stiffness of someone speaking a foreign dialect.

"Oh, fine," she assured him in a thoroughly unconvincing tone. "And you?"

"Could be better," he muttered darkly, avoiding her eyes again. He was looking around him, as if for an exit.

She'd forgotten that he was a shy man, at the core. She'd forgotten how sexy he looked with a sweat worked up. Many other things about him that she'd been forcing out of her mind were returning with a vivid, wrenching clarity. Lydie felt a warm throb of empathy for his discomfort that she immediately ignored, reminding herself that she wanted nothing to do with Justin Fuller.

"Well," he said with forced brightness. "Catch anything?"

Lydie looked at her fishing rod, then back to Justin, who was carrying one as well. Wasn't he supposed to be in Denver in a few hours?

"Justin . . .," she said dubiously, her throat suddenly tight with tension, "what are you doing here?"

"Good question," he muttered, raking a hand through his disheveled hair. "I thought I was keeping your grandfather company on a fishing trip. Seen him lately?"

"Grandpa?" She stared at him, confused. "No, I was with my father—"

She stopped, comprehension beginning to sink in. Lydie could see the same dawn breaking over Justin's face. For a long moment, they merely looked at each other. She wondered if her double-time heartbeat was loud enough for him to hear.

"Don't tell me," Justin began, a faint smile curving

the corners of his sensuous lips. "Your father convinced you to come along with him on a fishing trip,
and then, no sooner had you arrived than he . . ."

". . . had to go back to the car for some bait," Lydie
finished, unable to keep back a smile herself at the
absurdity of the situation.

"Could've sworn I heard a car drive off," Justin
mused. "Right after your grandfather disappeared on
a similar mission. He said he'd left his pipe in the
glove compartment."

"Grandpa doesn't smoke a pipe," she informed him.

"Oh." Justin nodded. In the silence that followed,
broken only by distant birdcalls and rustlings in the
underbrush, they both seemed to listen to the sound
of her father and grandfather's absence. Then Justin
cleared his throat and looked her in the eye more
directly.

"Crafty people, these Henleys," he said. "It seems
they wanted us to . . . bump into each other."

Lydie nodded. "So it seems." Her heart was re-
fusing to pipe down, booming in her chest with un-
diminished intensity.

"Why, do you suppose?" he asked quietly.

"I can't imagine," she said with a careless shrug.
She gave her hair a toss, chin raised in a perfect
posture of defiant indifference. It might have worked
well if she hadn't accidentally let go of her fishing
pole, which thumped to the wet ground, causing her
to give a startled jump.

The loss of poise was lethal. The next thing she
knew, Justin was at her side, and they were bumping
heads in an attempt to pick up the rod. Then it was
her hand he was reaching for, and his shoulder she
was steadying herself with, and somehow, before she

knew quite how it had happened, she was wrapped up in Justin Fuller's arms.

"Lydie," he breathed before his lips closed over hers, and her body pulsed to vibrant life, enveloped in the warm strength of him. She was hazily aware of his heart beating, as fast as hers, against her breast, and then a welling of confused emotions overpowered her.

She could only answer the urgent passion of his kiss with a desperate eagerness of her own, willingly surrendering herself to his powerful embrace. Her hands seemed to slide around his neck of their own accord as he pulled her closer, molding her body to his.

His tongue found hers, engaging it in a languorous, sensual, swirling dance. Her blood rose, breast tips swelling to aching arousal against the hard planes of his chest. His musky, masculine scent, the sweet-salty taste of him, the taut muscles that held her in willing captivity—all of it combined to sweep away all thought, all halfhearted protest. She wanted him so much it hurt.

She moaned his name in between fervent, frenzied kisses, her hands stealing over his shoulders, snaking through his wet, tousled hair. Justin's hands seemed to be touching her everywhere at once in a paroxysm of aroused excitement as their kiss deepened in intensity.

At last, with a shuddering breath, she broke away, gazing up into dark eyes that were hooded with passion. Leaning back in his arms, she could only shake her head weakly in wonderment, and his eyes glowed with amusement and affection as he gave a deep, throaty chuckle.

"Whoever said I had any brains in my head at all?" he murmured, his voice still husky with desire. "How could I have possibly stayed away from you this long?"

"I don't know," she muttered thickly. "I think I told you to."

"I shouldn't have listened," he growled, and he bent to plant a deliciously scalding trail of wet kisses along the line of her neck, stopping to nibble gently at the tender skin where her pulse throbbed.

Lydie let out a long sigh of pleasure, eyes half closing again. "I thought you were leaving," she whispered, unable to keep from moving sinuously against him as his lips nuzzled the hollow of her neck and shoulder.

Justin's face slowly rose, a look of reluctance in his eyes at having to leave this sensual feast of skin. "I was supposed to," he said, a shadow crossing his face. "It doesn't matter," he added with renewed forcefulness. "I'm here now."

"I'm glad," she whispered. "I've been miserable, you know."

"No," he said. "I didn't know. I thought you might be happier..."

"Fat chance," she muttered wryly, and he smiled, then gave the tip of her nose a gentle peck.

"I wonder if we could...find some drier land," he said. "And have a talk?"

Lydie looked down, realizing that although her rubber boots had protected her, Justin was up to his ankles in marsh water. "Good Lord!" she exclaimed. "You poor thing."

"No big deal. Just forgot to pack my rubbers," he said. "Do you have any idea where we might—"

"It's a very small island," she told him. "I was here

once before, when I was a girl."

Hand in hand, they made their way through the tall reeds to a rise where there was, finally, some solid ground. Under the cool shadow of a sheltering elm, they settled down together. Justin minus shoes and socks, and Lydie sans boots, they leaned back against the tree trunk, still unable to keep their hands off each other.

"Hey," Justin said, stopping her fingers as they ran restlessly over his thigh. "You've been painting again."

Lydie looked down at her blue-stained thumb. "Out of desperation—" she admitted, her words cut short by a sharp intake of breath as he lifted her hand, kissing and licking the tender skin between thumb and forefinger. "Careful," she whispered. "That's acrylic."

"Turns me on," he murmured, a mischievous gleam in his eye. "No, really, there's something about the smell of pain mixed with the smell of you . . ."

"I knew you were a weirdo," she sighed, leaning her head on his shoulder as he lowered her hand again, holding it in his lap. "Justin, I'm sorry I acted that way the other night—"

"You don't have to apologize. I never should have taken that phone call," he said vehemently. "I've been kicking myself ever since for not spending more time with you, right then and there. And I should have thought more before I spoke to you about your painting."

"No," she said firmly, sitting up. "You said the absolutely right thing. I *was* trying to cover myself up when I reworked that canvas. I was falling back into my worst old habit—thinking about what people might think . . . about what you might think. I'd exposed myself and I was starting to feel vulnerable."

"I love you exposed," he murmured, and there was a seriousness beneath the seemingly flip comment that touched her deeply.

"You do, don't you?" she whispered. "You believe in me. I guess that's why I was so supersensitive to your criticism. I wanted you to love what I did, unreservedly."

"I love *you*," he said simply. "The untouched-up, undisguised you. That's what I was seeing beneath the surface."

Lydie was silent, relishing the soft, supporting pressure of his hand enfolding hers. "Justin, I never realized you had a temper like that, though," she said quietly. "To tell you the truth, it was a little frightening."

"I did overreact," he began. "I'm really sorry if I—"

"No, you had some reason," she interrupted. "And I guess I overreacted to your reaction," she added with a rueful smile. "You see, the kind of argument we were having was too much like ones I'd been through with Martin. He always seemed to choose the magazine over me, but he'd get terrifically upset if I went off on my own."

Justin nodded, a sober expression on his face. "I did have reasons for being as upset as I was that night," he said. "But they were reasons that didn't really have to do with you." He paused, lips pursed, a troubled look in his eyes.

"Tell me, Justin," she prompted him gently.

He gave a little sigh and rose to his feet. "You remember what I told you about Joanne?" he said, looking moodily at his bare feet in the short grass.

"You felt you couldn't give enough of yourself to her," Lydie said. "You seemed to think it was your fault that things didn't work out between the two of you."

"Oh, it was," he said grimly. "Lydie, it's not easy for me to go into the whole thing, but I think you ought to know. I do owe you an explanation..."

She gave him an encouraging look, feeling confused but curious. Whatever it was that was troubling him, she had a feeling it couldn't break the bond they were forming together now.

"Joanne and I had been engaged, oh, half a year or more." Justin shoved his hands in his pockets, still looking at the ground. "We kept putting off the actual date—mainly because my projects were piling up, and I couldn't give much time to caterers and guest lists." He shook his head.

"Things got pretty tense between us after a while. Joanne wanted to pick the date and go ahead. She was nearly willing to elope, just so we could be married and get on with our lives." He frowned, his gaze shifting toward the blue water visible in the distance.

"I think she actually sensed we weren't going to make it," he said thoughtfully. "That's the ironic thing. Joanne was rushing ahead to marry, as if it were insurance or something. But we were starting to realize there were problems between us that wouldn't go away." He shrugged. "We were young, both of us. I keep saying that, as if to excuse us, but it is true.

"It all came to a head one night in late spring." Justin was pacing now, as if impatient to get through what was clearly a painful memory. "I was working on a grant proposal, knee-deep in papers and graphs and calculators. Joanne and I had a date to go over our plans—to actually decide when we would get married, and where." He sighed.

"I had to break the date. Sound familiar?" He shot Lydie one quick glance, then went back to his pacing, shoulders hunched, eyes downcast. "Joanne went nuts," he said grimly. "She'd had enough—enough procrastination, enough stealing me away from my work when I should have made the time to be with her. We fought. It was loud, ugly—awful. And then she ran out."

Justin's face darkened as he paused, staring into space. "I felt pretty bad, but I was still angry myself. I stayed right where I was. I finished the work I had to do, which took a lot of the pressure off." He grimaced. "I was just going to call her, ready to apologize and make amends, when the phone rang." His eyes met Lydie's. "It was the hospital."

"Oh, Justin . . . no," she murmured, feeling an anxious tightening in her chest.

"Joanne had been in an accident. She'd been driving around the campus—we were at MIT—letting off steam, and I guess she was driving recklessly. She ran a light, broadsided another car . . . They were calling from the emergency room."

Justin's face was ashen. Lydie wanted to reach out to him, even as the fear still tensed her body. "But she didn't . . . ?" she whispered. "You said . . ."

Justin shook his head. "Thank goodness, no. She survived. But her pelvic bone was shattered, her back severely damaged. She needed plastic surgery because of a cut on her face . . ." He exhaled a deep breath. "I won't go into the gruesome details, but Joanne spent the better part of a year in the hospital."

"Justin . . ." She shook her head helplessly, not

knowing what she could say.

"It threw her career for a loop, to say the least. But she was strong, and she got back on her feet." He held her gaze, his eyes seeming to shimmer with sadness. "Without me, after a while. The accident finished our relationship."

"But, Justin, surely she didn't . . . blame you."

"I blamed myself!" he exclaimed. "My God," he muttered, forcibly subduing hs voice, "I've never felt such guilt in my life. If I'd only this; if I'd only that—"

"It wasn't your fault." Lydie got to her feet and took hold of his arm. "You know it wasn't."

He shook his head. "Intellectually? Sure." Justin grimaced again, looking away. "But I couldn't help feeling responsible. For a while I stopped working. I even considered dropping out of the world altogether." He gave a rueful chuckle.

"I went off the deep end, briefly—and resurfaced. Hey, I was the one who had it easy—my scars were only psychic." He shrugged. "And then some friends of mine coaxed me back into action." He looked at her again. "I've been working ever since," he said quietly. "Working hard."

All these years, she mused silently, holding on to his arm, pulling him closer to her. And then the other night, when she'd run away—no wonder it had touched a nerve! Lydie felt her insides ache for him. The panic he must have felt, searching all over the peninsula for her . . .

"You had no way of knowing," he said gently, reading her thoughts in her widened eyes. "Like I said, I had reasons of my own for being upset. It wasn't your fault, really."

"Still, I'm sorry, Justin—so sorry," she whispered, and she clung to him, kissing his chin, lips, cheeks, trying in the best way she knew to erase the pain, to somehow make up for the ordeals he'd gone through.

Slowly, hesitantly, he lifted his arms to hold her. And then he did hold her, more forcefully, returning her kiss, melding his lips to hers with a searing force. She felt the power of their passion already overwhelming the bitterness and remorse.

She put all of herself into the kiss, joy welling up inside her as he responded, his mouth claiming hers with renewed desire. She felt his need match hers, the intensity building. Only after they were breathless with passion did they break apart.

His eyes sought hers, full of loving concern. "You don't think I'm some kind of monster, do you?" he whispered.

"Of course not," Lydie sighed. "I love you—the you inside," she added, echoing his own words.

"I was going to let you go," he said, eyes clouding again as he gazed at her. "I had my mind made up. From the way things were going between us, with me so busy and you needing more of me—which you had every right to need," he added quickly as she opened her mouth to protest—"I thought I'd have to give up any thought of trying again. I just seemed doomed to failure. But there was one problem."

"Which was?" she whispered.

"I couldn't," he said simply. "I'm too much in love with you. I don't care if I have to cut my workload in half, sell one company, step down off the board of another—throw my computer into Lake Michigan!" he went on, eyes lighting up with amusement at her look of horror. "You're worth changing my way of living, Lydie Henley. That's all there is to it."

"Don't be crazy, Justin," she protested. "I wouldn't ask you to do anything like that."

"I'm crazy already. Crazy for you," he said, hugging her to him. "I didn't realize I was still capable of having a good time until we hooked up. I'm spoiled now, Lydie. I want more."

"Justin," she said, reeling beneath his barrage of enthusiasm. "We're still just getting to know each other. I don't expect you to put your projects in jeopardy just because—"

"I want to watch more old movies," he said with comic gravity. "I want more popcorn to eat from your delicious sticky fingers. I want to go jump in a lake on a regular basis. I want to marry you."

"You . . . what?" She took a step back, not certain she'd heard him properly.

"Let's do it, Lydie," he said, smiling at her bewildered gaze. "You're the one who's given me lessons in loosening, in being spontaneous. Well, what we've got here is spontaneous combustion. And now I want to own the patent on this particular chemical reaction."

"You can't be serious—" she began, but her heart threatened to burst as she looked into his eyes and knew he was.

"Do I make you happy?" he asked.

She'd never been made so happy in her life. She couldn't deny it as she looked at him. And the thought of a future with Justin, a future she hadn't thought possible, filled her with an excitement that was overwhelming, even as her head whirled crazily with questions.

"Well, yes," she said. "But—"

"Gloriously happy?"

"Yes," she admitted, feeling a blush come over her as she saw the erotic implications gleaming in his eyes. "But, Justin—"

"Now listen, Lydie . . ." He was guiding her down beneath the shade of the elm again, cradling her in his arms. "I've managed to do quite a bit of thinking over the past few days. I was going to see you when I got back from Denver, but here we are now, and now hasn't meant as much to me in ages." He kissed her before she could say another word, and then held a finger to her tingling lips.

"I'm offering you quite an opportunity," he went on. "You can paint and paint to your heart's content, without having to survive on peanut butter and jelly sandwiches. You can hold down as many jobs as you want, of course," he added as she struggled to speak again. "I've kind of gotten used to running into you anywhere I go."

Lydie took a playful bite at his finger, and Justin shushed her with another kiss. "And every moment of the day or night that I don't absolutely have to be immersed in my work," he went on after reducing her to a mass of deliciously shivering nerves, "I'm yours— every bit of me. What do you think? Sound bearable?"

"I don't know," she said woozily. "I'll have to give this some serious thought."

"Don't think too much," he cautioned her. "It's bad for you." He bent down to capture her lips again, his hands moving over the thin material of her blouse to gently caress her already arousal-swollen breast.

"You mean . . . we'd be together, all the time . . . ?" she sighed, stretching out with voluptuous abandon as his circling fingers teased her skin to tingling life.

"We could be just like this," he said in a husky whisper. "Wherever you want to be. I do travel a lot, you know. You wouldn't get bored."

"Bored?" she murmured, pulling him on top of her, reveling in the feel of his hard length against her soft curves.

"You'll see," he murmured. "I'm going to love you with every inch of my heart and—"

Justin stiffened suddenly, his head jerking back. Lydie looked over his shoulder, startled to see the tail of his shirt rise into the air in seeming defiance of gravity. Then she saw the gleam of fishing line.

"Got me a big one," boomed a voice in the distance. "Will you look at the size of it?"

Justin, with an abashed smile, was trying to unhook the line from the back of his shirt as Lydie giggled, seeing the figures of Grandpa and her father approaching through the rushes.

"If that's my daughter underneath you, Justin Fuller—and I certainly hope it is," came her father's laconic drawl, "I hope you'll have the decency to cease and desist until you can get the proper license."

"Doesn't even have a fishing license," Grandpa scoffed. "He'd have to work pretty fast to come up with a marrying one."

"I'm working on it," Justin called, successfully removing the hook with a satisfying rip of shirt material.

"Seems so," was the muffled rejoinder from her father.

"Son, let's give 'em a break," said Grandpa, "and find us some trout in the meantime."

As their footsteps receded in the distance, Justin, laughing, gathered her in his arms again. "Darling," he whispered, hugging her close, "what do you say? Don't you think I'm making you a pretty good offer?"

"I guess," she said, snuggling up to him, her limbs once more comfortably entwined with his. "But I think I need more convincing."

"Convincing?" His eyes glimmered with a knowing look. He bent to savor her lips again, possessing her with a tantalizing sureness that made her blood simmer. "Like that?" he murmured.

"Umm," she sighed. "Convince me some more, Justin. I think I like this part the best..."

"I'll be glad to," he whispered. "Anywhere and always..."

SECOND CHANCE AT LOVE

COMING NEXT MONTH

SECOND CHANCE AT LOVE

Be Sure to Read These New Releases!